Warlocks

# ELEMENTAL FAITH

## L.M. SOMERTON

Elemental Faith
ISBN # 978-1-83943-821-9
©Copyright L.M. Somerton 2019
Cover Art by Erin Dameron-Hill ©Copyright December 2019
Interior text design by Claire Siemaszkiewicz
Pride Publishing

# ELEMENTAL FAITH

# Dedication

To falling under someone's spell.

# Chapter One

The view from Evrain's top floor office window at ThInk, the design company where he worked, was enviable. His drawing board was set up so that he got the best light in the building and could daydream whilst admiring Portland's cityscape and Mount Hood in the far distance. The rare sunny days were a gift. Today wasn't one of them and his view was nonexistent.

"I swear the weather here is worse than in Scotland." Evrain scowled at the scudding clouds and lashing rain.

"Talking to yourself again, Mr. Brookes?" Pete Markowitz, Evrain's office-mate, wandered over to peer at his work.

"How else am I going to find intelligent conversation around here?" Evrain grinned. "All you ever talk about is the Winterhawks or your latest conquest and I don't care about either."

"You know the boss put the two of us together in here for a reason," Pete said.

"Because we're both gay?" Evrain knew that wasn't the case but this was a familiar conversation and he was required to follow the pattern to keep Pete happy.

"That applies to half the staff here. It's because you're the only employee that knows squat about hockey and therefore will not dispute my opinions on the Hawks. I end up brawling with everyone else and that's not good for the office furniture budget, apparently."

"You don't have opinions, you make blinkered statements based on a relationship bordering on obsession. You're a hockey stalker, Pete, and you know it."

"You still have to listen and nod at my sage pronouncements. It's in your contract. Read the small print."

"Go back to work, you idiot. Or get me a coffee. At least that would be useful, and you don't appear to have anything better to do." Evrain stood back to examine the artwork on his board. The designs were to support the launch of a new perfume and lived up to every fragrance advertising stereotype ever created—exactly what the client wanted. "If I never have to use a shade of pink again, I won't object." Silence met his statement and Evrain realized he was speaking to an empty room. He hoped Pete had taken the hint about coffee and was making a trip to the independent coffee shop down the street rather than the vending machine in the staffroom, which dispensed brown-colored liquid of indeterminate origin. Evrain would rather drink some of Dominic's organic liquid fertilizer.

He took the opportunity provided by Pete's absence to use his power to manipulate some of the natural inks on his drawing, making subtle changes to the depth of the colors. The delicate work was difficult to manage with Dominic out of range. It was easier when Evrain could channel his power through his lover but he couldn't stash him in an office cupboard, however much he'd like to keep him close. He fiddled with the gold bracelet around his wrist. The heavy links pressed close to his skin and the clasp was robust. It wasn't a pretty piece and not worn for show. In fact, it was a little too similar to a manacle, something Evrain chose not to think about. Chains belonged on Dominic, along with an assortment of other bondage accoutrements, not on him, but the pure metal served to dampen his power, something essential to keeping the city of Portland intact.

Evrain's dick stirred at the image of Dominic chained naked to their bed. It wasn't a fantasy, it had been reality just the previous evening and Evrain couldn't wait to get back to his lover. He relished the challenge of turning him into a begging pile of need, with or without the use of his powers. "Perhaps I can get away with taking a few hours off this afternoon," he murmured. His current project was almost done and he'd been putting in a lot of extra time in recent weeks. His grandmother had left him enough money that he never needed to work again if he didn't want to, but he enjoyed the normality of having a career. Of course he *wasn't* normal and never would be, but sometimes it was nice to pretend. He pressed the heel of his hand to his crotch.

"Thinking filthy thoughts about Dominic again, I see." Pete elbowed through the door before shoving a take-out cup into Evrain's hand. "Can't say I blame you. If I had all that gorgeousness waiting for me at home, I'd have a permanent woody too."

"A woody? What are you, ten years old? And that makes me think of *Toy Story*, which is all kinds of wrong." Evrain took the coffee and mulled over a few ideas of how to get revenge on Pete. Not that he would act on any of them, but it was fun to imagine softening the tarmac so that Pete's car sank to its hubcaps in the street, or turning the cotton threads of his underwear back to their original plant form. "Now that one has potential."

"What does?" Pete asked.

"Just an idea for those science textbook covers I've got lined up as my next project."

"Right. I don't believe a word of it." Pete took a noisy slurp of his drink. "The three of us should have a night out soon. Drinks, dinner, hot, sweaty, shirtless dancing... You know the kind of thing."

"Nobody sees Dominic shirtless but me," Evrain growled.

"I know, I know... No need to get all dommy with me. He's not my type."

"He's everyone's type." Since Symeon Malus had worked his evil magic on Dominic, the man's beauty and allure were irresistible. Evrain would happily keep his lover locked away from public view but Dominic tended to get irritated if Evrain tried to prevent him from mowing his customers' lawns. Not that he did much of that work anymore, but he refused to give up a few of his elderly clients who relied on him the most. Those he was gradually handing over to a small start-up outfit he'd found, working with them until his favorite customers were content they could be trusted upon. Most of his work was now at Hornbeam Cottage, where his organic herb business was thriving.

"Show some pity. When we go out together you two attract all sorts of attention, which means I get to cruise the fringes of your admirers. I'm pathetic, I know, but I haven't gotten laid in weeks. I need you two to facilitate my sex life."

"I can name at least three clubs where you could pick up a one-night stand seconds after walking through the door," Evrain said. "You need to get less selective, that's all."

Pete stuck his tongue out at him. "How did you meet Dominic?"

"He was my grandmother's gardener, believe it or not. I helped him out potting a few seedlings and the rest is history." The truth was a lot more complicated than that but Pete didn't need the details and the part about potting seedlings was true.

"Unbelievable. Some people have all the luck." Pete went back to his own drawing board on the other side of the room, muttering under his breath. "Perhaps I should get a hobby, join a club or something. Flower arranging, or cake decorating."

"Then you're either after a nonexistent stereotype or switching sides. Without wishing to generalize, I think you'll find that most attendees at either of those classes will be female."

"Maybe I need a new girlfriend. She'd have better tips for hunting down a man than you do, that's for sure. Oh, I think your jacket's vibrating."

Evrain had turned his phone's ringer off during a staff meeting earlier that day. He retrieved it from his jacket pocket just as it cut off but when he saw who had called, he rang back immediately. "Dominic?"

"Hey. I'm sorry to disturb you, but is there any chance you can come home early?"

"Why, what's happened? Are you okay?" Evrain gripped the phone harder.

"I'm fine, but there's something here you should see. I don't want to talk about it over the phone. Don't worry— it's not dangerous. At least I don't think so."

"I'll be there in less than an hour." He disconnected reluctantly, a hard knot forming in his stomach. Dominic sounded scared and that was not to be tolerated. If there was even the remotest chance that he wasn't safe then Evrain had to be with him. "I have to go, Pete. If the boss wants my designs for the new perfume project, they're all here on my board."

"Sure, I can show him the poufy pink passion pong. Is everything...?"

"I don't know but I'll be in touch, okay?"

"Sure. Do what you need to do."

Evrain grabbed his jacket then ran for the elevator. He and Dominic had been living an uneventful, peaceful life for the last six months, something they had both enjoyed. "Should have known it was too good to last. Fuck," he yelled at the elevator doors, fear driving his temper. *I swear I'm never letting that man out of my sight again.*

\* \* \* \*

Dominic threw his phone into one of the armchairs in front of the fire. He hadn't wanted to disturb Evrain but at times like this he didn't have a choice. If he hadn't called and Evrain had arrived home to find what Dominic was now staring at, Dominic had no doubt that he wouldn't be sitting comfortably for at least a week. He brushed a strand of hair out of his eyes. "What do you think it means, Shadow?" He addressed his comment to the large, hairy black cat spread across the hearth rug. "Even in this household, *that* can't be normal." He stared at the sooty symbol that had appeared on the wall above the mantel. "I hope it's not dangerous." He was reassured by the cat's utter lack of interest. If the symbol was any threat to Dominic, Shadow would be herding him out of the door by now. She was almost as protective as Evrain.

Dominic checked his watch. It would be at least half an hour before Evrain got back from Portland. Not long enough to do anything useful in the garden, but too long to stand staring at black lines that meant nothing to him. He made a pot of coffee then sat at the kitchen table with one of Agatha's ancient gardening books. There was a big demand for saffron from the upscale restaurants in the city and Dominic wanted to try growing it. It appeared that saffron crocuses weren't a difficult crop to produce – the corms could be planted in summer for an autumn harvest. The local climate was going to be a problem though, because according to Agatha's book, the flowers needed reasonably warm and dry summers and autumns, although a little rain was fine. "We get more than a little rain here, Shadow, don't we?" The soil needed to be light, sandy and well-drained because saffron didn't tolerate heavy or wet ground. Of course, there were advantages to having an elemental warlock as a lover. Evrain could help with conditioning the soil, but weather control was beyond him for more than a short period – it took a huge amount of effort.

"The crocuses bloom in October, and you need to pluck the flowers and harvest the filaments as soon as possible after they've bloomed. The corms divide with the passing years, and you can separate and replant them to increase the stock. That's good." Shadow rolled onto her back, giving one paw a desultory lick. "You could pretend some interest, fur ball." Dominic read on. Though the crop was easy enough to cultivate, harvesting it was so labor-intensive that it would be almost impossible to make any profit from it. "It says here that the flowers have to be hand-picked as they bloom. The filaments – just three per blossom – have to be extracted then dried. It takes one hundred and fifty blossoms to make a single gram of market-ready saffron, and tens of thousands to make an ounce. Wow. I think I might have to restrict myself to growing enough to flavor the occasional fish stew. I can picture Evrain's face if I ask him to help hand pick crocus filaments – he'll get out that paddle with bumps on it." At the mention of fish, Shadow delivered an intense stare, lurched to her feet then ambled in Dominic's direction. She rubbed around his legs, head-butting his shins. He reached down to scratch behind her ears and a rumbling purr vibrated through his fingers.

"I suppose you want food. It's too early for your dinner." Shadow jumped into his lap and proceeded to knead his thighs with a set of needle-sharp claws. "Ow! Fine. You can have a few biscuits." Dominic knew he shouldn't give in so easily but once Shadow got an idea in her head there was no changing her mind. Her stubborn nature was something else she had in common with Evrain. "Let me up then." Shadow launched herself toward the cupboard containing her treats, meowing at the top of her voice. She was shoving her face into a bowl of biscuits when Evrain arrived, coming through the door with a gust of damp wind and a scattering of leaves. He slammed the door closed, paced across the room then took Dominic in his arms, marching him back until his ass hit the kitchen cabinets.

Dominic had seconds to draw breath before Evrain claimed him with a kiss, nipping at Dominic's lower lip hard enough to sting.

"You're okay."

"Of course I am." Dominic submitted to another punishing kiss, his cock plumping in response to Evrain's aggression. "Agatha had enough wards around this place to keep an entire battalion of demons out and she said they'd last forever."

Evrain cupped Dominic's cheek. "I worry about you."

"I know you do." Dominic gave him a shy smile. "Which is why I thought you needed to see our new décor in person." He gestured at the fireplace and Evrain turned to look.

"What in the ever-loving hell is that?" Evrain stalked across to stand in front of the fireplace. He reached for the graffiti above the mantel, not quite touching.

"It appeared just before I called you, not all at once but almost as if someone were painting it onto the wall. It smoked a little, then turned to that sooty color. Shadow wasn't bothered so I assumed I wasn't in imminent danger." At the sound of her name, Shadow glanced around, gave Evrain a narrow-eyed glare then went back to eating.

"That animal is nothing but a stomach on legs, but I trust her judgment where your safety is concerned." Evrain stared at the markings. "There's something about the symbol that's familiar. I can't quite place it."

Dominic joined him and Evrain clasped his hand, rubbing his thumb across Dominic's palm.

"It looks a bit Celtic to me. Are you going to call Gregory?" Dominic asked.

Evrain gave a pained sigh. "I suppose I must. He and Coryn should be back from their cruise by now. He'll insist on coming up here then he'll find excuses for more training."

"When will he consider you done?" Dominic asked, keeping the amusement from his voice.

"Knowing him, never. The man's a sadist. He takes enormous pleasure in demonstrating how much of a novice I am."

"Takes one to know one. Sadist that is, not novice."

Evrain pulled Dominic to stand with his back pressed to Evrain's chest. He slipped a hand down the front of Dominic's pants, cupped his package and squeezed. "And you love that about me."

"Evrain..."

"I've neglected you this week."

"Shouldn't you call Gregory straight away?" Despite his words, Dominic pushed back against the hard ridge of Evrain's cock.

"I'm entitled to a little rebellion now and again. I'll email him a picture of it. In the meantime, I think you should strip."

"Evrain...are you sure we're safe?"

"I don't sense anything evil about it at all. The wards are undisturbed and Shadow isn't bothered. I'm as sure as I can be. Now, don't make me tell you again, sweetheart. You're well overdue some discipline thanks to the hours I've been working and I'd be more than happy to apply my hand to your backside."

Shadow made a beeline for the door. She gave Dominic a baleful glare then began to scratch at the wood. "Hey, don't blame me." Dominic wandered over to unlatch the door. "I'm not the one upsetting your delicate sensibilities."

Evrain snorted. "Delicate, my ass. She knows I'll toss her voyeuristic, furry behind into the garden in a minute anyway. She's anticipating the need to evacuate the premises."

Tail held high, Shadow sashayed out of the cottage. Shaking his head, Dominic closed then latched the door. Evrain was snapping a picture of the new wall art on his phone.

"There. Knowing Gregory, he'll have the sound turned off on his mobile and won't notice the message for hours. Plenty of time for me to have my wicked way with you." He leered. "Why are you still dressed?"

Dominic shivered. He never failed to feel a frisson of excitement when Evrain was in a dominant mood. He still didn't understand why submitting to another man turned him on the way it did but he had learned to accept it. Evrain was a force of nature, kneeling for him seemed natural to Dominic — the way things should be. He took off his shirt, leaving his pendant in place. Only Evrain was allowed to remove it — fastened with magic and imbued with protection spells, Dominic couldn't take it off himself even if he wanted to. He touched the star-shaped black tourmaline wondering, as always, at its unnatural warmth.

"I'm getting impatient, sweetheart." The endearment didn't fool Dominic. Evrain's steel-edged tone held the promise of unavoidable punishment. "Raise your hands."

Dominic glanced up. There was an ancient iron meat hook embedded in the gnarled beam above his head, a loop of rough hemp rope hanging from it. As he watched, the rope unknotted in a sinuous slide and the vague ache he always experienced when Evrain channeled his power enveloped his body. He gave Evrain a narrow-eyed stare but lifted his arms, stretching his fingers toward the ceiling. In a snake-like dance, the rope wound around his wrists and the hook, tightening until he was forced to lift his heels from the floor. His cock hardened in response to his vulnerable position.

"You should have obeyed me quicker, love. I'm not good at waiting for what I want, you know that." Evrain circled him, tracing the lines of Dominic's muscles with the tip of his finger. He paused to unfasten Dominic's jeans, easing the zipper down with care. Dominic had forgone underwear that morning at Evrain's insistence. Now he whimpered as his aching cock bounced free.

"So beautiful."

Once past his thighs, the garment dropped to the floor.

"Step out of them."

Dominic shook the denim from his feet.

"I'll allow you to keep the socks on. The floor's cold and besides, they look cute."

Dominic rolled his eyes, but he was glad of the thick woolen socks. Flagstones suited the cottage, but the bits of exposed stone between faded rugs were always cold regardless of the season. He gasped and rose higher on his toes when Evrain gripped his cock.

"Nice and hard for me. Stay that way."

*As if I have a choice.*

"Any numbness or tingling in your hands?"

"No...Sir." Dominic flexed his fingers. The rope dug into his wrists but he didn't care — he craved the marks that would be left behind. Addressing Evrain with the honorific also helped put him in a submissive mindset, settling him in his skin.

"Good." Evrain ran his palm over the curve of Dominic's backside. "You'll tell me if anything hurts that shouldn't." The whimper that escaped Dominic's lips was involuntary. "Time to fill you up. You want that, don't you?"

"Please, Sir."

A shelf set in the side of the fireplace held Evrain's ever-growing collection of plugs and dildos. Gregory insisted that he practice manipulating natural materials and Evrain found it amusing to fashion stone and wood into tactile sex toys. Stone was much more difficult to work with than wood but so far Evrain had succeeded with quartz, polished granite and marble. He chose the quartz, his favorite, and the biggest of the bunch. Dominic's pulse sped up as Evrain coated the plug with a thick layer of lube, taking his time, making sure Dominic saw everything.

"You're enjoying this far too much." Dominic shivered in anticipation.

"What's not to enjoy? You're at my mercy—my favorite position for you. You're naked, the state I prefer you in, and I'm about to make you scream, which is always pleasurable." Evrain pressed the tip of the plug to Dominic's hole.

"Evrain..."

"Sir."

"Bossy warlock."

"Any chance you had of coming today is rapidly diminishing." Evrain pushed the smooth quartz rod into Dominic's channel. The stretch was accompanied by a mild burn that soon gave way to pleasure as Evrain nudged his prostate.

"Please. Please… Sir…"

"I love to hear you beg, sweetheart. Tell me what you want."

A small part of Dominic wanted to resist, a far larger part wanted to give Evrain whatever he demanded. "Touch me." The lack of friction on his cock was torment. "Touch me, Evrain, please… You're driving me mad." In response, Evrain pushed the plug in and out of Dominic's body, varying his pace and rhythm. "More. I need more." Dominic yanked on his bonds, attempting to push back so that Evrain would drive the plug deeper.

"Who's in control here?" Evrain withdrew the quartz rod to its tip.

"You are! Evrain… Sir… You, always you."

"That's right. Don't forget it. I decide what to give you, I decide between pleasure and pain." He thrust the plug deep into Dominic's channel. "You'll keep this inside you."

Dominic moaned. The plug was heavy, slippery — he clenched his ass muscles around the invader. In front of him, Evrain dropped to his knees. He swiped the end of Dominic's leaking cock with his tongue.

"Love the way you taste… Of herbs and green things, fresh like spring rain."

"Your Scottish accent turns me on."

"What accent?"

Dominic regretted saying anything if it kept Evrain's attention away from his cock. "When you're excited, or angry, you start rolling your 'r's… It makes me picture you in a kilt."

"I have one. The family tartan is very dark."

"Why doesn't that…oh!"

Evrain sucked the end of Dominic's cock, making it impossible to think until he pulled off with a pop. "You were saying?"

"You're evil."

"When it comes to torturing you, yes. Hundreds of years ago the family name was Brooke. Not sure where the 's' came from. So we use the Brooke tartan, which is mainly dark green and black." Mouthing Dominic's balls, Evrain hummed, sending vibrations through Dominic's body. He stopped again. "Would you like to see me in my kilt? I don't wear anything under it." He grinned.

"Can we save this conversation for later? Interesting though it is." Dominic worked his muscles around the plug.

"Or I could give you a potted history of tartan making. Did you know that one of the earliest examples of tartan found in Scotland dates back to the third century AD?"

"Evrain…"

"A small sample was found used as a stopper in an earthenware pot to protect a treasure trove of silver coins buried close to the Antonine Wall near Falkirk."

"Evrain!"

"So impatient." Evrain took Dominic's cock deep into his throat. He sucked hard and there was nothing Dominic could do to stop the orgasm that seared through him. Evrain sucked and swallowed until Dominic's skin was so sensitive he couldn't stand it any longer. He sobbed for mercy.

"Enough…please, Sir!"

Standing, Evrain gave Dominic's ass a sharp smack, jostling the plug. "I don't think I gave you permission to come."

"You're unbelievable." Dominic was glad of the bindings because he didn't think his legs would hold him up without the additional support.

"I am." Dominic shuddered as Evrain fondled his ass. "Unbelievably good to you, considering your lack of respect for my authority."

"Your...you arrogant...fuck me!" Dominic howled.

"Stop that." Evrain played with the plug some more.

"Once I'm done fucking you into unconsciousness, this is going back in. Gonna keep my seed inside you for the rest for the day."

"No! I..."

"You don't want me to fuck you?" Evrain feigned hurt.

"I didn't say that." Dominic whined. "I have to work."

"All *you* have to do is submit to my will." There was a rustle of fabric then the messy heap of Evrain's pants slid into view. He pulled the plug free and before Dominic could manage a yelp, pressed the head of his cock to Dominic's hole. "All stretched and ready for me. Nice and slick."

Dominic gripped the ropes holding him in place in an attempt to keep his body still but Evrain placed a hand on each hip, digging his fingers in hard enough to leave marks, keeping him steady. Dominic shivered then sighed his relief as Evrain pushed inside his body. The heat, the pressure, the fullness were all familiar and welcome. He floated on a wave of deep satisfaction. Evrain muttered and sparks tingled inside Dominic's body, as if Evrain's cock was coated with fireflies. Dominic gasped and danced from foot to foot.

"Be still." Evrain gripped him harder, ramming home his claim. Dominic gave in and let Evrain take control, not that he had much choice. Evrain nailed his gland over and over, sending him into a spiral of desperate need and acute pleasure.

"I love it when you give me everything," Evrain said, nibbling the nape of Dominic's neck. "Your powers of recuperation are remarkable." He licked Dominic's shoulder before pressing his teeth into the flesh just hard enough to sting.

"Evrain! Don't stop... Harder..."

For once Evrain didn't argue. He pounded Dominic's ass without mercy.

"I need..."

"You need what I give you." Evrain reached around Dominic's body to grasp his aching cock. He squeezed, harder than was strictly necessary, and Dominic came with a yell, his vision blanking. The sensations in his body were so overwhelming that his awareness of Evrain diminished to the point where they were joined and no more.

Evrain sank his fingertips into Dominic's hips, holding him close, sealing their bodies together as he came shouting Dominic's name. The gush of extra heat inside him made Dominic shake, his body attempting to come again even though it was impossible. He sagged in his bonds until the ropes slithered away from his wrists and he dropped into Evrain's secure hold.

"One of these days you're going to kill me with pleasure."

"Best to make sure that doesn't happen," Evrain muttered, half carrying Dominic to one of the armchairs next to the fire where he settled him onto his lap. "Because I intend to do that again and again and again."

"I should clean up."

"You should stay right where you are and besides, I'm going to plug you again before you shower — with something big, to keep you well stretched for me."

Dominic groaned. "Do you know how hard it is to work with one of those things inside you?"

"I don't have first-hand experience, so no." Dominic could feel Evrain vibrating with laughter.

"You're such an evil bastard. I thought it was part of the Dom rulebook that you had to try everything you do to me first?"

"I like to be the exception to most rules, sweetheart, as you've probably worked out by now." Evrain pulled Dominic close, fondling his softened dick. "I should cage this, keep it safe for me."

"What do you mean?" Dominic sat up, imagining all kinds of horrific scenarios.

"Chastity, my love. I could get hard just thinking about your sweet dick locked in metal for me. You would only be able to get hard when I permit it. I'd be the only person able to grant you release."

"No. Just no." Dominic's traitorous cock made an attempt to harden.

"You say no, but your body seems to be agreeing with me."

"I..." Dominic had no idea what to say. He couldn't deny that Evrain's words were turning him on, against his better judgment. His rambling thoughts were interrupted by the sound of a phone. He slumped against Evrain's chest. "Saved by the bell. Does Gregory know that you have the theme from *The Godfather* as his ring tone?"

Evrain shrugged. "I hope not." He reached for his cell. "Gregory, thanks for calling back. Did you and Coryn have a fun trip?"

"I think we can dispense with the niceties, Evrain. I can't leave you alone for ten minutes, can I?"

"What did I do?" Evrain rolled his eyes at Dominic. "I wasn't even here when the symbol appeared, I was at work."

"Well, you'll be glad to know it's benign. Nothing to worry about. In fact it will start to fade soon."

"I guessed as much because Shadow wasn't spooked. Dominic was here alone when it happened and that fur ball is more protective of him than I am."

Gregory snorted. "I doubt that. Regardless, I need to see you in person. Coryn and I will fly out today. We'll be there this evening and stay in your guest room."

"Why, what's up?"

"It's not something I can talk about over the phone, Evrain. We'll discuss it later, but for now I suggest you and Dominic check that your passports are in order." He rang off before Evrain could say anything further.

"What's going on?" Dominic wiggled into a more comfortable position.

"Apparently we'll find out later. In the meantime, I'm going to plug you, then we'll take a shower and start thinking about some dinner because we're going to have guests. Do you have a passport?"

"What?" Dominic was finding it hard to keep up. His mind had stalled on 'plug'. Evrain lifted him to his feet, giving his ass a pat. "I have you, sweetheart. Everything is going to be fine."

"Don't patronize me, Evrain. I'm a grown-up and quite capable of hearing the truth."

"The fact is I don't know any more than you do, other than Gregory said we will need passports. There's no point in worrying until he and Coryn get here and tell us what's going on. In the meantime, I can think of several interesting ways to take your mind off everything but me." Evrain stroked the curve of Dominic's backside, pushing his fingers between Dominic's cheeks to graze his hole.

"No chastity. No plug." Dominic glared at him even as his cock jerked.

"I don't hear your safe word, my love." Evrain took his hand and tugged him toward the stairs.

# Chapter Two

When Gregory, Coryn and Shadow crowded through the door of Hornbeam Cottage at eight that evening, the kitchen was the source of a wonderful, savory aroma. Evrain breathed in the smell, hoping that it might placate his growling stomach for a few more minutes. He nuzzled Dominic's neck before turning toward their guests.

"I was beginning to wonder what had happened to you two, it's late."

"Even private jets get held up in bad weather." Gregory handed Evrain his bag then gave him a one-armed hug. "It's good to see you, as always."

"Hi, Gregory, Coryn." Dominic waved a spatula. "Dinner won't be long, so I hope you're hungry."

Coryn dumped his bag next to the table before wandering over to Dominic. "Gregory ate about twenty bags of miniature pretzels on the plane. We are both famished and whatever you're cooking smells wonderful." He gave Dominic's shoulder a squeeze. "Is there anything I can do to help?"

"I just need to drain the vegetables. You could open a bottle of wine if you guys would like something to drink, or there's water or soda in the fridge."

"Gregory?" Coryn shrugged off his jacket, hanging it over the back of the nearest chair.

"A glass of white wine would go down well." Gregory leaned down to pet Shadow, who was winding in and out of his legs. "We were stuck at the airport for an age before the weather cleared enough for takeoff and my throat is drier than the Atacama."

"Because it's not like there was any water on the flight or anything," Coryn said, sarcasm oozing from every word.

"Not the point. I couldn't have a proper drink because we agreed I would drive here from the airport."

"Because you know the route better." Coryn took a chilled bottle of wine from the refrigerator. "Corkscrew?"

"On the table. You two bicker like an old married couple." Evrain grinned.

"That's because we *are* an old married couple," Gregory retorted. "Sorry, we're both tired. A good meal and a drink will fix that. Is the guest room set up?"

"It is. I'll take your bags upstairs while Dominic finishes up." Evrain carted the luggage and coats up to the spare bedroom, which he and Dominic had decorated in shades of lilac and silver gray. A deep purple embroidered quilt covered the bed and they had kept his grandmother's oak wardrobe and chest of drawers. The room was cozy once the lamps were lit and Evrain was pleased with the way they had managed to marry modern and antique. He grabbed some fresh towels from the closet on the landing to leave on the bed then went back downstairs, where

Gregory and Coryn sat at the table while Dominic dished up the casserole he had made.

"I know you're curious," Gregory said. "But let's eat first. We can talk over coffee."

"The symbol disappeared just like you said it would," Dominic said. "I'm glad Evrain saw it or I might have thought I imagined it." He took his seat. "Dig in, everyone, don't let the food get cold."

Gregory made sure the conversation turned to other topics. He and Coryn shared tales of their exploits on their recent cruise, which brought a blush to Dominic's cheeks.

"I can't believe you two. I'm surprised you didn't get arrested." Evrain sipped his wine, pushing away his plate. He patted his stomach. "That was amazing, love. Thank you."

"It's Dominic's herbs that make all the difference," Coryn said. "You're getting to be quite an accomplished chef."

The comment made Dominic blush even harder. He nibbled on his lower lip as he gathered up the empty plates to stack by the sink. "I made a cherry pie for dessert and there's ice cream to go with it." He slid the pie dish from the oven where it had been keeping warm.

"You're spoiling us." Gregory smacked his lips together. "Not that I'm complaining because... Pie!"

For a while the only sounds were those of happy munching as the four of them demolished their dessert. Even Shadow got a dish of cat milk so she didn't feel left out. She licked the bowl clean then settled on Evrain's lap, communicating her contentment through high-decibel purring. He stroked her, scratching her chin and behind her ears while Dominic made coffee.

When they were all settled with drinks, Evrain gave Gregory an expectant glance. "So, are you going to explain why weird magical graffiti appeared on our wall?"

Gregory drummed his fingers on the table as if trying to decide what to say first. Evrain reached across to take Dominic's hand.

"Have you ever thought about why we are the way we are?" Gregory asked.

"You mean, why we're warlocks?" Evrain said. It wasn't how he thought this conversation would go. Gregory nodded. "Of course I have. But I guess I just assumed that if there was some kind of explanation you or my grandmother would have told me. I suppose I thought we were anomalies. Some kind of peculiar offshoot of evolution."

"Well, that's not too far from the truth, to some extent," Gregory said. "There have been witches and warlocks throughout history — mostly dismissed as ignorant people seeking ways to explain things they didn't understand. But, as is usually the case, there's no smoke without fire. So many rumors and stories... How could they all be explained away?" Gregory sipped his coffee. "There are references going back hundreds of years to people apparently able to manipulate the elements. Think about it — Native American rain and sun dances, Wiccan fire spells, Naga the water deity who could supposedly control the weather...the list goes on."

"So you're saying people like us have been around a while?"

"Indeed. Well-hidden or hiding in plain sight but present on several continents for hundreds of years."

"And are you going to tell us why?" Evrain was getting impatient.

"I'm getting there." Gregory flicked his fingers and a spark hit Evrain's cheek. He slapped at the sting, scowling. "Respect your elders."

Dominic grinned and Evrain sent him a look that promised vengeance later, when they were alone.

"Throughout history, disasters have been averted through what has seemed like fortunate timing or coincidence. Elemental warlocks exist to maintain a balance. To stop evil overcoming the world. Our gifts have prevented or curtailed hundreds of incidents, some famous, some nobody's ever heard about."

"I don't understand." Evrain massaged his temples.

"That's because you're not using that brain of yours. Think about it." Gregory drummed his fingers on the table until Coryn laid his hand over them.

"Give the boy a break, love. He's still new to all this. You were once, you know. Many, many years ago."

Gregory lifted Coryn's hand to his lips for a soft kiss. "You're right, of course. It wasn't that long ago!"

"Of course I'm right." Coryn glanced across at Dominic. "We mere mortals often are."

"Sorry. Sorry, Evrain. I'm being a grumpy old man."

"Nothing new there," Evrain muttered, but he smiled. "My brain clearly isn't working so how about you give me the idiot's guide to warlock history?"

"Think of a time in the past when the elements have altered the course of events," Gregory said.

"I think I should have paid more attention in class," Evrain muttered.

"The Spanish Armada," Dominic contributed. "In 1588 the Spanish attempted to retreat from the British, but unseasonal, violent Atlantic storms threw them off course, and dozens of Spanish ships were lost."

"It's gratifying to know that at least some young people appreciate their education these days. Well done, Dominic, that's an excellent example," Gregory said. "Can you think of any others?"

"Um..." Dominic frowned. "How about the Battle of Long Island in the Revolutionary War? If I remember, after days of fighting the British, Washington decided to cross the East River and withdraw. He started the ferrying process at night, but by morning a large part of the army was still on the wrong side of the river. Had the British seen them, they likely would have been killed or captured but a dense fog concealed the activity. By the time the fog lifted and the British charged, the Continental army was gone."

"Very nice example. If Washington had lost those men, it's highly possible the war could've turned out differently. There are so many examples — in 1274 and 1281 Kublai Khan's Mongol fleets failed to conquer Japan because two major typhoons destroyed his ships. The emperor claimed he had summoned the 'kamikaze' — or divine — winds to save Japan. Hitler and Napoleon both suffered major setbacks because of extreme weather. The Great Fire of London never spread into Westminster, which it could easily have done, and despite the huge damage, very few people died. I could go on."

"So you're saying our ancestors had a hand in controlling the elements, but what about all the disasters — earthquakes, volcanoes, tidal waves?" Evrain asked.

"There are limits to our powers, Evrain. How difficult is it for you to pull water through rock? We'd hardly be able to avert a major earthquake once it was underway. However, there are instances when they've been delayed to limit casualties. Forest fires can be shifted, floods redirected, but it takes huge effort. Not every warlock is capable of such extremes—we all need to understand our limitations."

"Why do I have a feeling this is heading somewhere I won't like?" Evrain's trepidation increased, causing his stomach to cramp. He poured more wine into his empty glass, trading it for his coffee.

"It's happening very early. You're far too young and inexperienced."

"What is?" Evrain's frustration was beginning to get the better of him.

"The test." Gregory's piercing stare made Evrain straighten in his seat. "The symbol that appeared on the wall is a call to take a test that every warlock is subjected to once they have found their life partner. I was in my mid-forties when it happened to me, a long time after I'd met Coryn."

Coryn rolled his eyes. "The symbol appeared on the bedroom wall while we were...well, I'll let you work that one out. It put a dampener on proceedings, I can tell you."

Dominic snickered. "I'll bet."

"Could we get back to the whole 'test' thing? What is it, exactly?" Evrain massaged his temples.

"I don't know," Gregory said.

"What do you mean, you don't know?"

"The test is different for each individual. I have no idea what yours will be. I do, however, know where you need to go because it always happens in the same place...and you must leave immediately. Your response to the call is part of the test. Those who have ignored it have found their powers gradually diminish…it's as if they were found wanting…not to be trusted." Gregory shook his head. "Such arrogance. Just because we don't understand how or why this happens doesn't mean it can be ignored. Warlock histories, scant though they are, are very clear — the test is a warlock rite of passage. Even Symeon Malus obeyed the call."

"What about Nate?" Dominic asked.

"It hasn't happened to him yet because he hasn't found his life partner…though I doubt it will be long before Damon is recognized as such."

"What was your test, Gregory? If you're allowed to talk about it of course." Evrain stood, his chair too confining.

"He had nightmares about it for years," Coryn said. "It wasn't fun, though my memories of what happened are hazy."

"While mine are as sharp as if it had happened yesterday," Gregory muttered. "Part of the process — the partner is protected, to a certain extent, while the warlock is traumatized enough that the lessons learned will never be forgotten. Perhaps it isn't such a bad thing that you've been called young. Your self-discipline may improve as a result."

"You're scaring Dominic, love. Get on with it," Coryn scolded.

"Coryn was taken from me, kidnapped if you like. I had to follow a set of clues to find him. He was chained to a pole in the middle of a circular forest clearing and as I approached, a ring of fire ignited around him. All very dramatic."

"And warm," Coryn added.

"Quite. There was no obvious water source to put out the flames. I manipulated the air, but it didn't work so in the end I shook the earth, liquefied the ground until the flames were swallowed, but that wasn't the end of it. A tornado formed with Coryn at the eye, the loosened rock and debris I had created got caught up in the spinning wind. I fought to control it, to hold it in one place, knowing Coryn would be flayed if it touched him."

"Jesus Christ! I'm not sure I want to hear any more." Evrain stood with his hands on his hips. "If this is what we've got to look forward to I'm not getting on a plane to anywhere."

"You're not listening. This isn't optional, Evrain. Unless you want your powers to fade over time, you *will* do this. With your strength you have the potential to do a lot of good. I for one don't want you to waste your talent."

"But if it puts Dominic in danger…"

"You're a partnership. Anything you do in the future depends on Dominic. He's a part of you now."

"I could go alone…"

Gregory hissed his frustration. "Don't be so stubborn. You go together or not at all. Now do you want me to finish telling you what happened or not? Jesus, sometimes I want to put you over my knee…"

Dominic and Coryn were both trying to hide their laughter. "Alpha male warlocks are a constant source of entertainment," Coryn spluttered. "Honestly, they are as bad as each other."

Dominic nodded his agreement. "I want to hear what happened," he declared, "if the two of you could stop arguing for five minutes. What did you do, Gregory? How did you save Coryn?"

"Well, like I said, I was fighting for control and getting tired. It was hard to concentrate but I realized that I had to think outside of the immediate problem and look for something that could help me. Coryn was tied to a wooden stake. I reminded the oak what it was to be alive, coaxing branches from the central pillar. The branches broke the path of the whirlwind and it dissolved. After that, there was an eerie calm and absolute silence for a few minutes. When the birds began to sing again I realized that the test was over."

"And I woke up in his arms," Coryn contributed. "Not that I'd been deeply asleep, just not fully aware of what was going on. It's still vague in my memory, like a half-remembered dream, all I can recall is having absolute trust that Gregory would do whatever he needed to."

"The whole thing sounds terrifying," Dominic said. "You're sure there's no way out of this? Evrain hasn't been a fully-fledged warlock for very long, it doesn't seem fair."

"Once the symbol appears, that's it. Your path is set and the only decision is whether or not to accept the challenge." Gregory swallowed the last of his coffee then gestured for Coryn to pour him another. "If there was anything I could do about it, I would, but this is bigger than you or me, Evrain. Did you recognize the sigil?"

"It looked familiar," Evrain said, "but I couldn't place it."

"Check the cover of the family bible some time."

"Of course! It's embossed in the leather, isn't it?"

"Yes. Warlocks have been seeing the same thing for a very long time. Not that it has anything to do with religion of course."

"Someone has to organize the test, I assume. Who?"

"A senior warlock gets the call in the same way you did—though it's a different symbol. It's a bit like warlock jury service. You may never be called or it may happen more than once. It's considered an honor…and the more inventive the test, the better."

"Have you ever been called?" Dominic asked.

"Not yet, no."

"I don't like the idea of some other warlock having this kind of control over my life," Evrain said.

"It's not the other warlock that has control of the situation, it's a much older power that I don't pretend to understand. He gets a boost from ancient magic so that the test is suitably demanding."

"I'm still getting used to what I am and what I can do. I don't want to lose it—it's part of me. It's who I am." Evrain felt guilty for saying what he was thinking.

"And I wouldn't have you any other way," Dominic said. "You wouldn't be you if you weren't a warlock. Wherever we have to go, I'm coming with you. We face this together."

"Good, that's decided." Gregory took another slurp of his coffee. "I feel a sudden need to get hammered. Is there more wine?"

Chuckling, Dominic retrieved a fresh bottle from the refrigerator. "When will we have to leave, and where are we going?"

"I think we can afford to give you a day to sort everything out, but you'll need to leave the day after that. You'll be going to Scotland."

Evrain stared at him. "I was expecting you to say we had to go to some remote corner of the planet, not back home."

"The place you need to get to is in the Cuillin Mountains on the Isle of Skye, not your family's backyard. Though, if all goes well, you should be able to fit in a visit home while you're over there. Your mother would string me up if she ever found out you'd been in the country and hadn't stopped by."

"You and me both," Evrain said.

"You mean I have to meet your parents?" Dominic looked a little pale.

"We are facing a test that could result in death for one or both of us, and you're worried about meeting my mum and dad? I think you need to work on your priorities, love." Evrain ruffled Dominic's hair.

Dominic gave him a sheepish smile. "It's a big thing. I've only ever spoken to them on the phone."

"And they love you already, so you have nothing to worry about." Evrain refilled his glass. "There's so much to organize. We can't just jump ship on a whim — we have lives here, obligations."

"Coryn and I will help you work everything out. We'll stay here at the cottage until you're both back from your trip. It's too late to make any plans now. Why don't the two of you go on to bed? Coryn and I will clear up the dishes and we'll reconvene in the morning."

"I'm not sure I'm going to be able to sleep," Dominic murmured.

Evrain put his glass on the table and an arm around Dominic shoulders. "I think I can find a way to wear you out, sweetheart. Life with me was never going to be boring, was it?"

Dominic pushed his chair back. "I like boring. Boring is good."

"Good night, you two," Evrain said. "Everything you need is in the guest bedroom. We'll see you in the morning." He steered Dominic toward the stairs. "Maybe this is just a dream sequence like in one of those bad soap operas Gran used to watch."

"We can only hope. You know she only watched those things to ogle shirtless men, don't you?"

"Well she wasn't using them for intellectual stimulation, was she? And they always seem to find some very hot actors... I can't believe we're talking about daytime TV. We really must be desperate to avoid the topic in hand." He tugged Dominic into the bedroom and began to relieve him of his clothes. "We'll be discussing the weather next." He was a lot happier with the situation once he had Dominic naked and spread-eagled on their bed. He kicked off his shoes then straddled him, admiring the view that belonged only to him. Dominic's eyes sparkled and he nibbled on his lower lip.

"What do you intend to do with me?"

"Anything I damn well please." Evrain licked a path from Dominic's sternum to the hollow at the base of his throat. "Any objections?" He took the incoherent response as willing compliance.

# Chapter Three

After fucking Dominic into an exhausted sleep, Evrain lay listening to his lover's even breathing, envious that he couldn't find the same peace. His thoughts were in turmoil and even the joy of bringing Dominic to an orgasm that had made him scream hadn't been enough to calm Evrain's mind. He twisted the gold bracelet around his wrist, the snug fit not allowing much play. Its dampening effect wasn't enough to hold back the power building within him. He needed to vent and it wouldn't wait until morning.

He lay still for a few minutes longer, wanting to make sure that Dominic would remain asleep and get the rest he needed, then rolled out of bed. He pulled on underwear and a pair of pajama bottoms that rarely got any use. Focused on each other, neither he nor Dominic had thought to pull the curtains and now the moonlight streamed through the window, illuminating the bedroom and highlighting the edges of the dark wooden furniture with silver. Dominic's head was turned toward the wall, leaving his copper hair bathed in light. It glimmered each time his breath caught a few of the strands, enhancing Dominic's ethereal beauty even more. Evrain's heart pounded as he watched. He couldn't bear the thought of taking Dominic into a situation where he might be hurt. He felt backed into a corner, trapped, and it was making his blood boil. For a second he thought that might be literal, his skin felt dry and hot and, despite being shirtless, it was tempting to open the window for a blast of cold night air.

With a final glance at Dominic's sleeping form, Evrain padded from the room then made his way downstairs to the kitchen. Curled in one of the chairs next to the fire, Shadow twitched an ear. An emerald-green line flashed as the cat half opened one eye. Apparently deciding that sleep was far preferable to vacating her cozy spot, Shadow stood, stretched, did a couple of rotations then resumed her position.

Evrain grinned, thinking that a spoiled cat's life wouldn't be half bad. He was almost at the cottage door when the slightest sound alerted him to someone else's presence. He turned to find Gregory at the foot of the stairs.

"You need to vent, don't you?" Gregory walked toward him.

"My skin is too tight and the bracelet isn't helping. I need to let off some steam or things are going to start exploding around here."

"Emotional turmoil doesn't help your control. I'll come with you."

Evrain nodded, happy to have his godfather's company. "I'd like that." Still barefoot, he followed the grassy path to the back of the cottage then passed through the gate to the adjoining field. He traversed the huge boulder that Gregory often used in his training, making his way to the stream at the field's boundary. As he walked, gusts of wind swirled through the grass at his feet and a scattering of leaves lifted into the air. When he reached the stream the normally placid waters churned and boiled. He spotted small, golden fish leaping into the air as they escaped downstream.

"They know where they're better off," Gregory mused.

"Can you make sure the water is clear?" Evrain said. "I don't want to kill anything."

"Sure." Gregory muttered under his breath as he twisted his fingers into several peculiar shapes. "It's all yours. Even the tiniest microbe has now vacated the premises."

"Thanks." Evrain flexed his hands. It wasn't necessary to raise his arms and make dramatic gestures, but Evrain found it easier. Without Dominic to channel his power, focusing on the movements helped him hold on to control, albeit by a very delicate thread. Venting wasn't something Dominic could help with, which Evrain was grateful for—channeling was painful enough for Dominic and the kind of power Evrain was about to release had the potential to cause the love of his life serious harm.

Evrain took a few deep breaths and slipped the gold bracelet from around his wrist. He stuffed it in his pocket then, closing his eyes, he stretched his arms toward the water and stopped trying to hold back his power. Fire flooded his body, issuing from his hands in a single wide stream. When it hit the water, clouds of steam rose into the air until he and Gregory were concealed by the resulting fog. He shuddered as the power coursed through him, every muscle and sinew strained. He cried out in pain, the venting taking much longer than it usually did. When the pressure finally eased, Evrain dropped to his knees, his head bowed. His chest heaved as he tried to suck in some much-needed oxygen.

"That was…extreme." Evrain shook his head in an attempt to clear his clouded vision.

"You left it too long, didn't you? That, combined with the shock of finding out about the testing, meant that the build-up of your power was more severe than usual." Gregory squeezed his shoulder. "Are you feeling better now? I think you sucked every bit of heat out of the surrounding area."

Evrain nodded. He fastened the gold bracelet back around his wrist. "It seems like I need this all the time now."

"I'm not surprised," Gregory said. "You're so powerful, the dampening effect of the gold is the only thing making it bearable for you. I'd suggest a second bracelet for your other wrist and perhaps a chain to put around your neck."

"Slave bands," Evrain muttered. "I want to control the power, not the other way round."

"Don't be so precious. They're just tools and they work, which means you have to put up with them. I'll get another bracelet made and have it ready for you when you return from Scotland."

"You're confident I'll pass this test then?" Evrain struggled to his feet, starting to feel the cold now the venting was over, especially as he'd lowered the ambient temperature by a few degrees. The knees of his thin pajama bottoms were soaked through and the light sheen of sweat that coated his chest chilled his skin. He took a few shaky steps in the direction of the cottage.

"Of course. I'm not going to pretend that it won't be challenging for you, for both of you, but you're in love and committed to each other. That will help."

"And you're absolutely certain it has to be both of us? I don't want Dominic hurt."

"It's a test of your partnership as well as your power. I'm afraid there's no way around it. Both of you have to go, both of you will face the test, albeit in different ways." Gregory tramped across the field. "Believe me, I understand your reticence but this will only happen once in your lifetime. Once it's done, your status will change and you'll get the chance to use your abilities for good."

Evrain sighed. "It would have been nice, after everything that happened with Symeon and then Imelda and her coven, to have a bit more time to spend with Dominic before heading into another drama. He's already suffered so much because of me. Held captive, his appearance altered, the tattoos beneath his skin… So much pain and all because of me. He'd have been better off if he had never met me."

"Self-pity isn't becoming in a young warlock. You're talking rubbish and you know it. You and Dominic were made to be together." Gregory gave him a clip around the ear.

"Hey! Stop that!" They'd reached the cottage door.

"Only if you stop whining."

"I'm not whining, I have legitimate complaints."

"Go take a shower, Evrain. We'll talk in the morning." Gregory shook his head before making his way back to the spare room. Evrain watched him go with a heavy sigh. Gregory never gave him an inch.

A shower *was* a good idea, though. Evrain's feet were filthy and he was shivering from the cold. He went upstairs to the bathroom, set the water running then stripped off his sodden pajama bottoms. He braced his arms against the sink, bowing his head. Now he had vented, fatigue crept over him. The door creaked open and he looked up to find Dominic frowning at him, his expression a mixture of sympathy and frustration.

"You should have told me you needed to vent—I would have come with you. I don't sleep when you're not in the bed anyway."

"There was no point in the two of us getting cold and miserable. Gregory came along to give me a few home truths as well, not something you needed to hear."

Dominic shrugged out of the striped bathrobe he wore. "It's nothing I haven't heard before," he said. "You're a bit blue—this hot water is going to burn like hell."

Evrain pulled him close until they were pressed together chest to groin. "I feel better already."

"Fuck, you're freezing." Dominic wrestled free then clambered into the shower. "Get in here."

Evrain did as he was told, yelping when the hot water made contact with his chilled skin. He submitted to Dominic's attentions as he was soaped and shampooed, the heat soaking into his cold muscles. "Feels so good."

Dominic turned off the spray and within a couple of minutes they had both toweled dry. "Bed. And no going anywhere without me for the rest of the night."

Beneath the covers, Evrain pulled Dominic close until his lover's ass nestled into his groin. He slipped an arm around his waist, imprisoning him.

"Did you burn anything down this time?" Dominic murmured.

"No. I did fuse some of the streambed into glass, but it looks kind of pretty."

"You must have generated a serious amount of heat to do that." Dominic sounded worried.

"I let it build too long. Gregory's already given me a verbal smacking, I don't need it from you too."

Dominic gave a low snort. "I'm glad he's around to tell you off, you deserve it."

"Unless you want a spanking, go to sleep," Evrain growled. He tightened his grip on Dominic's slender body. "I'm too tired now but in the morning I'm going to turn your ass pink."

"Promises, promises…" Dominic's voice softened and soon gentle snores told Evrain that he had fallen asleep. This time Evrain stopped resisting the pull of darkness.

* * * *

Despite the disturbed night, Evrain woke early. The curtains had remained open and the dawn light targeted his closed eyes as if seeking revenge for past evil doing. "Oh God," he groaned. "It can't be morning already."

Dominic grunted but remained stubbornly asleep. Evrain massaged his temples, a headache already building. He should have drunk a glass of water before bed — venting always dehydrated him. His tongue was sandpaper in his mouth and his lips were sore and cracked. He didn't want to leave the warmth of the bed but thirst drove him out. He was halfway to the door, stark naked, before he remembered there were guests in the house and he didn't want to give Gregory or Coryn an eyeful. It was way too early for the sarcastic comments he knew he'd receive so he grabbed Dominic's robe, paid a quick visit to the bathroom then headed down to the kitchen. His route to the coffee maker was booby trapped by a hungry, impatient cat deliberately getting in his way and yowling for attention.

"Anyone would think you hadn't been fed for a month." He bent to stroke Shadow's dark head. "Greedy animal. You're a walking stomach, aren't you?" He got an indignant look and a few flicks of Shadow's tail. "All right, all right, I get the message." He spooned tuna from a half-finished can into a clean dish. "Looks like you'll be pampered for a while. Your uncles will be taking care of you while we're away. Jesus, why am I having a conversation with you? You're not taking a blind bit of notice." Shadow had her head buried in her dish, loud chomping noises transmitting her pleasure. Somewhat jealous that Shadow could take such enjoyment from a simple bowl of fish, Evrain set about making a pot of strong coffee, which was his equivalent first thing in the morning. He was sitting at the table, hands wrapped around his mug, when Coryn made an appearance.

"Oh God, give me some of that." He lurched toward the coffeemaker. "You had a late night last night."

"Sorry... I didn't ask Gregory to come with me."

"I know, the stubborn old man seems to think you still need babysitting. I don't know what the two of you got up to, but he was in an exceptionally good mood when he came back to bed."

"Don't tell me anything else," Evrain said. "I don't want to know. As far as what we got up to, I needed to vent. Gregory helped me avoid frying any of the local wildlife then decided I need a pep talk and a clip around the ear for some reason."

"Sounds about right." Coryn joined him at the table, his silver hair tousled. Evrain hoped he looked as good when he reached Coryn's age. "I don't have to tell you, do I?"

"No." Evrain sipped his coffee, the bitterness reflecting his mood. He knew exactly what Coryn was talking about. "I love him so much, Coryn. I'll take good care of him."

"There's a fragility beneath Dominic's strength, Evrain. He needs you. You're part of each other even more than Gregory and me and we've had so many more years together, so much more experience. Dominic will be frightened, however much he hides it, and it's up to you to provide the reassurance he needs." Coryn blinked. "Of course, if he had any idea I was suggesting such a thing to you, he'd have my hide. He doesn't want to be a liability, but sometimes it's easy for you warlocks to forget that your partners are simple mortals, with mortal vulnerabilities."

"I won't forget."

Coryn nodded, closing the subject. "I'll start some breakfast. After last night, Gregory is going to have quite the appetite."

Evrain chuckled. Shadow jumped onto his lap and began to puncture his thighs. "I'm more into administering pain than receiving it, Shadow." Evrain tapped a velvet paw. Shadow did a few circles before settling, only twitching an ear when Coryn laid a few rashers of bacon in the frying pan.

"I'm sorry you're having to uproot your life for us again," Evrain said.

"I'm quite looking forward to it, actually," Coryn replied. "Florida is hot, wet and full of snakes… And not just the reptilian kind. Here it's cold, wet and the wildlife still wants to kill you but is more direct about it. I also enjoy gardening and I'm going to love taking care of Dominic's herbs for a while. I dabble at home but it's not the same. It'll do Gregory good to be away from the business for a while, though he has interests in this corner of the world, as you know. He'll no doubt be plaguing the life out of the management at ThInk."

"I hope he has a damn good cover story ready for me because I've taken enough time off from work already."

"Family emergencies happen. How many eggs would you like?"

"Two please. Dominic gets them from one of his clients who has her own hens and they taste a hundred percent better than any other eggs I've ever had."

"The happiest, most pampered hens on the planet." Dominic, wearing faded, ripped jeans and a cream sweater, made a beeline for the coffee. "I smelled bacon. Somebody stole my robe so I had to get dressed."

Evrain's cock twitched. His body never failed to respond to Dominic's presence and he now regretted not dressing before coming downstairs. Shadow gave him a baleful glare before jumping to the floor.

Dominic bent to pet Shadow, presenting Evrain with the perfect view of his denim-wrapped ass. He was grinning.

"Brat," Evrain murmured under his breath. "You know exactly what you're doing, don't you? You're overdue a spanking, something I should have administered this morning." Dominic's slow smile told him that the attention would not be unwelcome.

Gregory's arrival shifted Evrain's thoughts to less stimulating topics and he forced himself to think about everything that needed to happen before he and Dominic could leave for Scotland. There would be plenty of time to deliver punishment once this new, unwelcome challenge was over and they were both safely home. Two transatlantic flights would give him ample time to think up something appropriate.

# Chapter Four

Three days later, Evrain negotiated the heavy traffic heading out of Edinburgh before driving toward the north-west of Scotland. After almost twenty-four hours' traveling, he and Dominic had spent their first night in a hotel that nestled in the shadow of Edinburgh Castle. First class flights ensured they had traveled in comfort but sleep had evaded Evrain as his mind obsessed about what they might face over the coming days. Dominic's tension had been evident, though he had done his best not to show it.

In Edinburgh, exhaustion had overtaken him and he had slept with Dominic wrapped in his arms, seeking the comfort of skin on skin contact. After a hearty breakfast, which Evrain had forced down because his body needed the fuel, they had stowed their luggage in the back of the Range Rover they'd picked up from a rental company at the airport and begun their journey.

"I hope we have a chance to come back to Edinburgh and see the sights before we fly home," Dominic said. "Though I suppose you've seen them all before."

"I'd love to play tourist and show you around if we have time. Edinburgh is one of my favorite cities. There are the obvious things to see like the castle and Holyrood, but I could take you to places that the average tourist doesn't get to know about. Nelson's Monument on Calton Hill and the botanic gardens if the weather's good. If this test goes well, we can spend a few days meandering back, taking in a visit to the family on the way."

"Your mom is going to kill you when she finds out you've come over without letting her know we were making the trip."

"I don't want her to be disappointed if we don't make it home for whatever reason."

"I know, but she's still going to beat you." Dominic's tone suggested that he was looking forward to the spectacle.

"We have a long drive ahead through some spectacular scenery. That doesn't mean I won't be taking note of every comment you make that merits punishment," Evrain said.

Dominic shrugged. "You'll be too jetlagged to do anything about it for a while."

"And that's two already. Keep it up." Evrain hid his smile.

"Where are we staying tonight?"

"Changing the subject won't help you, but we are on our way to a small hotel on the waterfront in a place called Plockton."

"Cute name. Sounds like something out of a kids' TV program."

"I suppose it does. It's a pretty place and the hotel has great views of Loch Carran and a reputation for fantastic food. I want us to be well fed and rested before we cross the bridge into Skye tomorrow morning."

"The last supper... I'm not sure I'll have much of an appetite." Dominic turned away to stare out of the window, hiding his expression.

"I sincerely hope it won't be our last. It's a shame we're not here for pleasure. I have a feeling we won't be able to appreciate the spectacular scenery quite as much as we would if we were on holiday."

"Well, we'll deserve some vacation time once the rough bit is over."

"I'm hoping that the anticipation of what's going to happen is much worse than the reality." Evrain reached over to give Dominic's thigh a gentle squeeze. "You didn't sign up for this, love."

Dominic turned to face him, his eyes glistening. "I signed up for you and everything that comes with you. I didn't expect that living with a warlock would be dull, though I also didn't imagine it would be quite as exciting as it has been so far, but I'm not going anywhere. Deal with it."

"Are you discovering a latent dominant streak?"

"Uh, no. Hey, wow, there's a ruined castle up there." Dominic twisted to look out of the back window.

"There are around two thousand castles in Scotland so that won't be the last one you spot."

"Two thousand!" Dominic gaped.

"That's just the ones built between 1100 and 1600."

"How do you know this stuff?"

"My dad's a walking, talking trivia quiz. He's also a history professor, remember. I don't recall a childhood holiday that didn't involve scrabbling around castle ruins. We'll see Eilean Donan tomorrow—it's spectacular."

Dominic grabbed his phone. "I'm going to look it up, then see if I can read about the Cuillins. A bit of background research can't hurt, can it?"

"No, it can't." Dominic's innocent enthusiasm gave Evrain a bad case of the warm fuzzies. It was at times like this when he couldn't quite believe how lucky he was, that a man like Dominic would give him the time of day let alone stand by him through thick and thin. He focused his attention on the road in an attempt to block out all the 'what ifs' fighting for space in his mind. He didn't think mitigation strategies came into play for a warlock test. There was no way he could predict what might happen.

Dominic gave him a running commentary on all the information he was reading on his phone until he had to plug it into the car charger. Evrain smiled and nodded in the right places but didn't take much of it in—it was enough that Dominic was occupied rather than worrying about the next few days. They stopped for lunch at a roadside café housed in a converted train carriage, eating quickly and leaving with thick slabs of fruit cake and paper cups of strong coffee. Once the roads got quieter, Dominic took a turn driving so that Evrain could rest his eyes. Dominic had never driven a stick shift before but took to it like a natural, proclaiming it to be much more fun than an automatic even if he did have to drive on the wrong side of the road.

By early evening they were within an hour of the hotel and Evrain's stomach was rumbling. After a brief discussion, they decided to press on and eat when they got there. They swapped seats again, so Evrain was at the wheel when they finally pulled in to the hotel car park in Plockton. He turned off the ignition then indulged in a long, groaning stretch, easing the kinks from his body. "That's the farthest I've driven in a long time. I think I need a three-hour massage using at least half a bottle of baby oil."

"You can't just come out and say that kind of thing when we have to be around people," Dominic said. "Now I'm imagining your body all slick and shiny with oil."

"I packed some."

"Some what?"

"Baby oil. I thought it might come in handy." Evrain kept a straight face even though he put way too much emphasis on the word 'handy'.

"What else have you got in your suitcase that I don't know about?" Dominic asked, his cheeks a little flushed.

"Let's just say the guys manning the X-ray machine at the airport got quite a show." Evrain opened the car door. "How about we go inside, get settled and fed, then I show you?"

Dominic sank his teeth into his lower lip and pressed the heel of his hand into his groin. "I hope the restaurant service is quick."

The receptionist's hair was a far brighter shade of red than Dominic's and she had a scattering of freckles across the bridge of her nose. She grinned as they approached the desk.

"Mr. Brookes, Mr. Castine... You're my last check-in of the day. I hope you had a pleasant journey."

"Thank you, yes," Evrain said. "It's been a while since I've been in this part of Scotland."

"Well, welcome back. You have the lake-view suite on the second floor." She handed over a key. "Would you like any help with your luggage?"

"We can manage. Do we need to make a reservation for dinner?"

"No, I'll just let the restaurant know that you are on the way."

Evrain thanked her even though he wanted to smack her for ogling Dominic, something she wasn't attempting to hide. They had a double room so she had to know they weren't platonic roommates, but that didn't seem to bother her. Evrain shook his head and grabbed Dominic's hand. "I can't take you anywhere, can I?"

Dominic gave him a perplexed look. "What are you talking about?"

"The receptionist wants in your pants. I feel the need to remind you who you belong to."

"I didn't notice anything."

"No, you never do...roll with it, I'm feeling possessive."

"And this is a change from the norm how?" Dominic hefted their bags into the elevator, which was an old-fashioned cage type. He heaved the inner door into place with a clang. "No one gets in my pants but you, you know that." He pushed the button for the second floor and the elevator rumbled upward.

"A chastity device is getting more and more tempting," Evrain muttered under his breath. "She was stripping you in her mind, I know it."

"Maybe she was just pleased to have a kindred spirit in the hotel...you know, another redhead," Dominic said as they piled out of the elevator. He picked up both bags so that Evrain could tackle the key to their room.

"Inside, brat." The spacious suite consisted of a large bedroom, complete with half tester bed, modern bathroom and a separate lounge area with a flat screen, couch and minibar.

"This is great," Dominic said, exploring.

"Only the best for Gregory. I have to admit it was very generous of him to pay for this entire trip. He didn't need to, but he said there was a special account set aside for warlock business that had built up over centuries. He said this occasion was exactly what the fund had been designed for and that we deserved some comfort on the journey."

"Limousine to the airport, first-class flights, amazing hotels... If only this were just a vacation and we could really enjoy everything. I said that already, didn't I?" Dominic sounded wistful. He sat on the side of the bed, bouncing to test the mattress. "This is so comfortable." He yawned. "If I weren't so hungry, I'd be tempted just to go to bed."

"Well, the sooner we eat the sooner we can test its resilience. I'm going to freshen up. Could you get a clean shirt out of my bag for me?"

"Sure."

Evrain freshened up in the bathroom. Splashing cold water on his face helped to wake him up because though it was only early evening, his body hadn't yet adjusted to the new time zone. Discarded shirt in hand, he wandered through to the bedroom to find Dominic stretched out on the bed, sound asleep, Evrain's clean top next to him. Evrain marveled, as always, at how beautiful his lover looked, the dark red waves of his hair tumbling around his face. He gave up on the idea of dinner in the restaurant and, after redressing, grabbed the room service menu instead. Dominic needed to rest—a more limited meal selection was a small price to pay.

Evrain let reception know they would be dining in their room then placed an order with room service. The twenty-five-minute wait would give Dominic a decent power nap. Evrain stretched out next to him, smiling when Dominic turned toward him, snuggling closer.

"My sweet man, I love you so much. I'm not going to let anything, or anyone, hurt you." Evrain sighed, wishing he could make the whispered words a promise.

He was nudged from half-sleep twenty minutes later by a knock at the door. Their food had arrived on a trolley, which the waiter wheeled into the room.

"Just leave it outside in the corridor once you're done, sir." He departed with a smile and a nod.

"Dom, sweetheart. I need you to wake up now." Evrain gave Dominic's shoulder a gentle prod. "I can't eat all this food on my own."

Dominic stirred, blinking his way into consciousness. "What's going on? Did I fall asleep?"

"Just a bit." Evrain chuckled. "You were away with the fairies when I came out of the bathroom so I ordered room service. I didn't think you'd fancy a trip to the restaurant."

"Sometimes you make excellent decisions." Dominic sat up, rubbing his eyes. "Must have been more tired than I thought. I'm hungry though. What did you order?"

"Seafood pasta with garlic bread, chocolate mousse with strawberries and a bottle of sparkling mineral water. I didn't think it was a good idea to drink alcohol tonight, tempting though the idea is."

"That all sounds so good." Dominic clambered from the bed then went to explore the trolley. "Smells wonderful." He began sorting the dishes onto the table so that they could sit to eat. Evrain gave a wry smile at the moment of domesticity but took his seat at the table without saying anything. The meal passed in companionable silence—neither of them had ever minded the quiet—they communicated with appreciative moans and the clatter of forks on empty plates.

"Wow, that was good." Dominic licked the last of the mousse from his spoon. "As far as last suppers go, we couldn't have hoped for better. My appetite clearly isn't bothered by impending doom."

Evrain shook his head. "If you're trying to provoke me, you're doing a fine job. You licked that spoon with way too much enthusiasm. We've just eaten, so I'm not going to put you over my lap. Hands and knees, on the bed... Oh, and get naked first." Evrain wondered for a moment if Dominic might refuse but he pushed his chair back, a slight smile lifting the corners of his lips. "Was I bad?"

"Why do I think I've just given you exactly what you wanted?" Evrain watched from his seat as Dominic took his time stripping off his clothes. He was already erect. "Wait. Stand there a moment." Evrain got up then walked across to his bag. He rummaged beneath the clothes until his fingers closed over cool metal. "This should ensure you don't come until I want you to. Hands behind your back." Evrain fastened a heavy iron ring around the base of Dominic's cock and balls, making them stand out in a lewd, enticing display. "Better." He gave Dominic's ass a tap. "Onto the bed, sideways on."

"You're a cruel man," Dominic muttered as he got into position.

"Yes, I am."

"No warlock stuff tonight?"

"No, I don't want to alert anyone to our presence unnecessarily. I have no idea who might be able to feel my use of the power." Evrain stroked Dominic's backside, dipping between his legs to finger his plump balls. "Besides, every now and again it's nice to do this without magical assistance, don't you think?" Before Dominic could answer, he spanked him hard, admiring the red handprint he'd created on his pristine skin.

Dominic moaned and wriggled to get more comfortable, resting his forearms on the bed, his head dipped toward his arms. Settling his stance, Evrain delivered a rhythmic series of firm blows, spacing them across butt cheeks and thighs. Dominic whimpered, pushing his ass back in an invitation for more.

"Harder, please, Sir. I need it."

"It's for me to decide what you need." Evrain administered a few more spanks. He tested the heat of Dominic's skin with the backs of his fingers. "Spread wider. Good." Evrain strolled to the bathroom to fetch the lube from his washbag. When he returned, Dominic's shoulders were trembling so Evrain calmed him with a gentling hand on his lower back. Quickly, he stripped off his clothes before unscrewing the cap on the lube. After coating two fingers with a glistening layer of gel, he stroked them over Dominic's hole.

"Please, Sir... Please."

The formal address sent a shiver of pleasure down Evrain's spine. He applied more lube then thrust his fingers into Dominic's receptive body, feeling for the nub that would drive Dominic wild with need. When he hit his target, Dominic's back arched and he groaned. Evrain played a little more, enjoying the heat and tight grip of Dominic's inner muscles. Between

Dominic's legs, his stiff cock and swollen balls were flushed. A glimmering sheen of perspiration coated his skin and Evrain couldn't resist. He licked Dominic's salt-sweet ass.

"You're killing me." Dominic's voice was strained.

Evrain coated his cock with lube, the touch torment to his sensitive skin. He lined himself up with Dominic's hole, at first pressing just the tip of his shaft inside Dominic's body.

"Dammit, Evrain... Stop teasing me."

"Patience, brat." Evrain thrust forward. It was all he could do not to come instantly. He took a couple of deep, calming breaths before jacking his hips. He couldn't sustain an even rhythm — there was too much sensation. He gripped Dominic's hips and drove into him again and again, his orgasm overtaking him with a ferocity that shocked him. He pumped his seed into Dominic's body, claiming him, owning him. The desperate need to mark him was overwhelming. Dominic panted and gasped, making the sweetest whimpers, and when Evrain finally relaxed, Dominic collapsed, rolling onto his back. Evrain unfastened the cock ring before straddling Dominic's limp body. He plunged his mouth over Dominic's rigid cock, letting it hit the back of his throat before sucking hard then digging the tip of his tongue into Dominic's slit. Dominic yelped and came in a gush, his limbs jerking. Evrain swallowed every drop and, after a few more leisurely licks, flopped next to Dominic.

"Wow." Dominic grabbed Evrain's hand.

"That about sums it up," Evrain said. He turned to give Dominic a thorough kiss. *I hope that wasn't the last time.* He kept his thoughts to himself. "I'm sticky. Let me get a flannel." After a quick trip to the bathroom and an even quicker clean-up, he nudged Dominic beneath the covers and spooned behind him, placing a protective arm around his waist. "Sweet dreams, love." Dominic's mumbled response told Evrain he was already halfway to sleep.

# Chapter Five

Evrain awoke to the sound of a howling wind tearing through the glen. His palm burned and he clenched his fingers, smiling at the memory of the reason for the ache. The realization that Dominic wasn't in bed beside him dawned slowly and for a few short moments Evrain clung onto the hope that he was in the bathroom. The silence told him otherwise. He got out of bed, reaching for his clothes, cursing.

"If he's gone for a fucking dawn walk without telling me, I'm going to kill him. Well, maybe not kill him, but punish him. A lot." Clad in jeans and yesterday's shirt, he shoved his bare feet into his deck shoes, lacing them with fumbling fingers. "Dammit, Dominic... Where are you?"

Too impatient to wait for the elevator, he jogged down several flights of stairs then pushed through the door into reception. The desk was unmanned, not surprising considering the hour. A vague clinking of crockery and cutlery came from the direction of the dining room where Evrain assumed they were making the final preparations for breakfast service. The main door was unlocked but it took some force to open it against the wind.

"Fuck." Evrain regretted not putting on a jumper as cold sliced through him. He knew instantly that the storm wasn't natural. His emotional agitation would mean that the elements around him would be in turmoil, but he had nothing to do with the gale or the choppy surface of the loch. It was so murky he couldn't see the opposite shore. He reached for his power, but nothing happened. He could feel it, still there below the surface, but there was a disconnect between it and his ability to use it. The sensation made him nauseous, so he stopped trying.

Cursing, he ran toward the water, a thick mist rising around his knees. Before he reached the shoreline, a torrential downpour came from nowhere, soaking him to the skin in seconds. Knowing it was futile but with a driving need to do something, Evrain jogged half a mile up the loch, searching for any sign that Dominic had been there. He retraced his steps and did the same in the opposite direction but there wasn't the tiniest clue to Dominic's whereabouts. It was as if he had vanished from the face of the planet. Evrain screamed his frustration into the wind, the sound lost, shredded. Fisting his eyes, reasoning that his tears were due to the wind and rain, Evrain made his way back to the hotel. The receptionist, a young man rather than the girl from the previous evening, looked at him askance.

"Get caught in the rain, sir?"

Evrain scowled at the inane question. "Good guess. I'd like to extend my room booking for two more nights. I'm heading over to Skye for the day and may not be back this evening, but I want to leave our luggage here and come back the following day. Would that be okay?"

"Let me just check the booking system." After tapping a few keys and peering at his computer screen the receptionist smiled. "That will be fine. Would you like the room serviced, sir?"

"No, we've hardly used anything, so there's no need." He didn't want anyone poking around their stuff unnecessarily. He intended to leave as soon as he'd dried off and changed his clothes. In his heart he knew that Dominic was long gone. How it could have happened, he had no idea. Dominic had been taken from right next to him, from their bed, and he hadn't heard a thing. As the elevator took him to the second floor, he allowed himself a sigh of disgust. Despite his vow to keep Dominic safe, he had been caught unprepared. He'd failed, though he got the feeling that he could have chained Dominic to the bed and he still would have disappeared. Forces were in play that were far more powerful than Evrain could ever hope to be. The best he could do would be to face whatever trial was planned as fast as possible in the hope that it would bring Dominic back to him.

Evrain took a quick shower then packed a small rucksack with a change of clothes for Dominic in case he needed them and a couple of bottles of water. He intended to travel light and move fast. He texted Gregory, giving him a very brief update on developments. His phone rang seconds after the message was delivered.

"What the heck time is it there? I didn't mean to wake you," Evrain said.

"My lack of sleep is hardly important." Gregory sounded grumpy. "Things are moving fast. Be careful,

Evrain. Guard your temper, stay calm. Provoking you is part of the test."

"I can't reach my power at the moment. How the hell am I going to be able to do anything useful?"

"It will return, I'm sure. They've stolen the love of your life — they don't want you blazing a trail across Scotland with your warlock histrionics. This is about you and you alone, not exposing our kind to the rest of the world."

"I hope you're right. It's not a comfortable feeling."

"Focus on the practical things you need to do — getting from the hotel to the location on Skye. It's rough terrain. You won't be able to get very close in the car, even with a four-wheel drive, so be prepared to hike. The isolation is deliberate, not only for privacy but because there will be limited resources on hand to help you. Dominic won't be harmed, Evrain. They need him. Taking him this early ensures your compliance."

"It's like somebody has torn a hole in my heart... It hurts."

"Your souls are intertwined. You need each other and separation is always difficult."

"I need to go."

"I've got faith in you, Evrain. We both do. Coryn sends his love too. You'll get through this, I know you will. You're stronger than you know and I'm not just talking about your power. Call me as soon as you can."

"I will." Evrain ended the call with some reluctance. Even so far away, Gregory provided much-needed support. Alone, Evrain felt uncertain and ill-prepared. After one last look around the room, he left, skirting the edge of reception to avoid conversation with anyone. Once in the car, he programmed the GPS with the coordinates Gregory had given him before the trip then, gripping the steering wheel far too hard, headed toward the Skye Bridge.

Evrain drove on autopilot, paying just enough attention in the slippery conditions to avoid an accident. The driving rain continued as if there were magnetic attraction between the car and the clouds. In the rear-view mirror, the sky was clear blue. In the distance, the black, towering peaks of cumulonimbus threatened a storm of epic proportions. Unpredictable weather wasn't unusual in Scotland so no one would bat an eyelid at the sudden changes happening around them, they'd just shrug and either put on or remove their raincoats according to need.

Grateful that the roads were quiet at such an early hour, Evrain reached the Skye Bridge in good time. He paid the toll then crossed, not even glancing at the waters of Loch Alsh. In the distance the Cuillins loomed, dark and foreboding, wreathed in a mantle of cloud, their jagged tips hidden from view. Only the hardiest hikers would be out and about in such appalling weather—Skye's mountains were not forgiving to unprepared amateurs. Dominic's research had revealed that several people had died amid the sheer slopes and crevasses over the years. Evrain repressed a shudder, wondering how many of those fatalities had been warlocks attempting the test. Gregory had refused to tell him how many of their number had failed and perhaps it was better not to know.

After narrowly avoiding a sodden sheep ambling across the winding road, Evrain gave himself a shake. He didn't want to run the car into a ditch and not even make it to the grid reference he'd been given. He wouldn't be much use to Dominic if he was trying to extract himself from the mangled wreckage of a car crash.

He followed the satnav until tarmac turned to gravel and the final bit of furrowed track ended at the listing, rusted gates of what appeared to be an abandoned quarry. He pulled the car over to one side so that it was partially hidden behind a stand of thick gorse bushes, then turned off the ignition. Listening to the rain pounding on the windscreen got him nowhere, so he pushed his seat back to give himself room to change into sturdier boots than those he was wearing. He wriggled into his waterproof coat, deliberately chosen for its dark gray color. With his black cargoes, his outfit should help him merge with the landscape, which was a blur of slate and granite. There was no phone signal, yet the route-finding app worked, showing him the staccato line of a footpath that wound around the back of the quarry into the mountains. Leaving everything but his phone in the car, Evrain ventured into the rain. Wind sliced through him, dagger-edged and frigid. He tightened the toggles on his hood and snapped shut the collar that came up high enough to cover his mouth. Water beaded on his lashes and the few strands of hair not protected by his hood were instantly plastered to his face. He flexed his fingers, wishing he'd remembered to bring gloves.

If he'd thought it would do any good, Evrain might have screamed and shouted but he needed every breath for the scramble up the side of an uncooperative mountain. He had to cross one ridge, traverse the valley then find a route through what appeared to be sheer rock. The footpath petered out after a mile or so, by which time his knees were already battered from crawling over the shifting scree. The mountain seemed determined that he should take two steps back for every one forward. There was little grip and his fingertips were raw from grasping at sharp rocks. He fell several times, cursing under his breath at each newly acquired bruise and scrape.

It had been six hours since he'd discovered Dominic's disappearance. In that time the forces of nature had conspired to turn him into an exhausted, battered shell. Resting for a moment at the side of a tarn, its ink-black waters churning, he reached for his power once more. To his amazement, the connection had returned and relief overwhelmed him. He dropped to his knees with a sob, dragging in deep, ragged breaths. The thread of energy that connected him to Dominic was there, still strong, meaning Dominic was alive and well. Though Evrain knew deep down that Dominic wouldn't be harmed, he needed the reassurance of certainty.

With fresh determination, he pushed on. Scree gave way to jagged, ice-smooth rock, slick with rain. Coarse vegetation ripped at his trousers, finding skin. He brushed water from the screen of his phone, praying it wouldn't give up on him. The map showed ever narrowing contours, impossible terrain and no way across the next range without a ton of mountain climbing equipment. He squinted into the rain, looking for any clue to where he could go next, but he was faced with sheer rock. Scrambling closer, he skirted massive fallen boulders to take shelter beneath a tangled thorn bush contorted into a twisted shape by the wind. He leaned against its trunk, panting, staring at the map on his phone. Then the screen went blank.

"Fuck!" Shaking it proved fruitless, so he shoved it in his coat pocket. "Think, you idiot. Think." The grid reference of his final destination seemed to be inside the mountain, which made no sense at all. Gregory had done his test in the open air so Evrain had assumed his would be the same. He was well away from prying eyes — even the sheep steered clear of this inhospitable area. Evrain extended his senses, testing the structure of the rock. He waggled his fingers, trying to ease their cold stiffness, then pushed with a gesture toward the mountain. It seemed solid, no caves or concealed gorges. The cold was dulling his senses so he drew a little stored warmth from the earth.

"The quarry... Perhaps it's not a quarry at all, but a mine!" Talking out loud helped clear his thoughts. The excavated ground he had passed through after leaving the car could easily have been the head of a mine. He directed his power at the earth in a different direction, this time probing beneath his feet. He closed his eyes as an image built of passages and larger open spaces. "Yes! It is a mine. But how do I get down there?" He didn't want to go all the way back to where he'd started. The first two access shafts he identified had been filled in with loose rock and boulders then capped with concrete. With his senses directed below ground, he lost his footing and tripped over a stray branch. He decided sitting was safer. He was already wet through, so a bit more water wouldn't make much difference. Cross-legged on the ground, he closed his eyes and let his senses wander, tracing the myriad dead ends beneath the earth. He sought traces of metal, hoping to locate a ladder to the surface. The iron of an abandoned tool glowed bright in his mind, small dots could be nails or sheared bolts. The first ladder he found reached only halfway to the surface before meeting a blockage while the second had him crying out his success. He had no idea whether it would be sound enough to use, but if his elemental sight was true, the ladder should grant unimpeded access to the mine workings.

He scrambled to his feet, maintaining a view of the ladder's rough location. It wasn't that far away but he'd never have found it by accident. Concealed beneath vengeful brambles, the shaft was covered by a rusted grid, which lifted clear with an angry, grinding protest. Evrain sucked on a deep scratch on his hand and stared into the darkness. The part of the ladder he could see was red with rust, some of the rungs missing. It was pitch black and he needed light. He couldn't create fire from nothing so he searched for luminescent material, finding some lichens with potential. He encouraged them to glow, sending silent thanks as a dim light illuminated the shaft.

He had no more reason to delay so he set boot to rung and began a descent that made his heart pound, afraid that at any moment he would be sent hurtling to a nasty end. His luck held and he breathed a sigh of relief when he reached solid ground. There was barely enough light to see by so he groped his way along the passages, finding that only one route remained clear. Traces of power suggested another warlock had passed this way and Evrain couldn't avoid the feeling that he was being herded in a direction of someone else's choosing. If it took him to Dominic, he didn't care.

He couldn't detect the signature of human warmth but another warlock could easily shield people with a simple manipulation of the air. All Evrain could do was follow the path. He guessed more than an hour passed before he felt the whisper of wind on his face and natural light overtook luminescence. He walked into a boulder-strewn clearing surrounded on all sides by sheer cliffs but open to the sky. Over time the roof of a mined cavern must have collapsed, leaving behind a landscape that could have been on another planet. In its center, perhaps two hundred yards from where Evrain stood, Dominic lay unmoving on a rock slab, the stone manipulated to form bonds over his wrists and ankles, holding him in place. Evrain ran to his side, overwhelmed by relief that he'd found him but fearing that he'd been hurt. Dominic wasn't even wet. He was deeply unconscious and protected by a thickened blanket of air.

"Evrain Brookes, welcome to your testing." A deep voice echoed around the hollow. Evrain's eyes were drawn to the rim of the cavern where a hooded figure stood near the edge. The light was behind him, creating a glowing halo around a dark shape. "I hope you're familiar with fairy tales because I've taken my inspiration for your trial from some of them. Your partner is very beautiful, isn't he? A real sleeping beauty."

Evrain shuddered, casting anxious glances around him.

"Don't be concerned—he is well, and will remain so if you succeed. If you do not...he won't suffer."

"Leave him alone... It's me you're testing." Evrain's voice carried without him needing to shout. The acoustics of the exposed cave funneled sound.

"It is, and it's time to begin. I suggest you focus." The mysterious warlock stepped out of sight. Evrain guessed he couldn't be far away, presumably with his partner, but it didn't matter. With Dominic unconscious, the playing field was set and Evrain would have to make the best of it.

# Chapter Six

Evrain reached for Dominic's arm, wanting to feel the warmth of his skin, but as he did, thorn bushes sprang from the earth. He had to move back or be impaled by the three-inch spikes that covered every gnarled stem. Like Triffids on steroids, the bushes grew until the barrier towered above Evrain's head. They surrounded him, pressing closer and closer until he had no room to move. Thorns penetrated his clothing, piercing skin. It took the pain to spark him into action. He wouldn't be any help to Dominic if he turned into a pin cushion.

Summoning his power, Evrain felt beneath the earth, seeking out the roots of the shrubs. There was too much moisture stored in the stems to stop their growth that way, he had to resort to more extreme measures. He manipulated the structure of the earth, binding granules together, crushing the roots. Earth wasn't his strongest element but Gregory had made him practice with it the most. Never had Evrain been more grateful for his godfather's dogged persistence in training him, even when he protested like a spoiled brat. He wondered how much of that persistence had come from knowing about the test to come and how it might play on Evrain's weakness. He focused, blanking all other thoughts to concentrate on the minerals beneath his feet. A thorn stabbed into his upper arm, driving deep, and for a few seconds he thought he'd failed. He applied more pressure, shifting the earth to his will, pressing the roots to pulp. He raised an arm to protect his eyes. A barb scraped his cheek then slowed, and gradually withdrew. He suppressed a yell as the spike in his arm pulled free, taking ragged breaths in an attempt to calm his racing heart. That had been far too close for comfort—he needed to anticipate better, react quicker. He had been distracted by his fear for Dominic. It had made him sluggish. He couldn't afford to let it happen again. He suspected the warlock testing him would have no compassion for weakness born out of love.

Within five minutes it was as if the thorn bushes had never existed. Evrain took a single step toward Dominic and the heavens opened, dousing him not with rain but hail. Using a trick from his nemesis, Evrain thickened the air over his head, gaining some protection from the beating he was taking, until the wind changed direction, hurling pea size pellets of ice into his face. He closed his eyes, grasping with his mind for the threads of the wind, trying to wrest control from the other warlock. To his shame, he channeled, hoping that Dominic wouldn't be able to feel what he was doing. He needed fine control for what he was trying to achieve, not the wild flashes of power that inevitably resulted when he didn't use Dominic as his conduit.

A distant rumbling registered and he realized that the hail had been a distraction. A painful, annoying one but hardly life threatening. He should have grasped that the test was nowhere near severe enough and now he had given the other warlock time to activate his next surprise. The rumbling grew to a thunderous roar then, from behind him, water cascaded over the rim of the crater. The waterfall knocked Evrain from his feet, sweeping him thirty yards or more. His shoulder glanced against a boulder and he gasped as pounding water blinded him. It was freezing, chilling Evrain to the bone. He struggled to rise, falling twice as water swirled around his knees, rising to thigh level in less than a minute. He had to duck beneath the flood in order to push up with his hands and surfaced, spluttering, as he surged to his feet.

He couldn't sense the source of the water to stop it, so the only course of action he could think of was to give it somewhere else to go. He had never forced the full extent of his power into the ground and feared that he might lose consciousness if he did, but he could see no other way. Cursing, he flexed his frozen fingers and brought his will to bear on the earth, rending it apart. A jagged crack opened at his feet, zigzagging its way across the floor of the hollow. The noise of falling water was overtaken by the scream of the earth as it wrenched open, exposing a deep crevasse. Water poured into the hole, disappearing into the depths of the earth, draining away to leave a slick layer of mud.

Evrain dropped to his knees, his vision swimming. There were no pretty stars or tweeting birds flying in front of his eyes, just a dark red haze that resembled blood-infused fog. He vomited, the acid contents of his stomach mixing with the mud.

"Fuck." He spat, attempting to clear the foul taste from his mouth. It was a small mercy that Dominic was unconscious and unable to feel the full force of the channeling Evrain had had to employ. The pain must have been extreme.

Evrain crawled toward Dominic's rock bed — it was beginning to resemble a sacrificial altar in his head. There was no change in his condition. He looked serene, peaceful and far too young. Evrain whimpered, missing the strength Dominic lent him. Until that moment he hadn't realized how much he relied on Dominic's quiet certainty in his abilities. It was selfish to want him awake, to give encouragement in the calm, low voice he always used when Evrain was emotional, or strung-out on power.

At that moment, Evrain wasn't sure he could muster the energy to extinguish a candle flame, let alone complete the test. He was exhausted, soaked and battered bloody. His thorn-stabbed arm throbbed. The hail had eased but the rain still fell, monsoon-strength and bitterly cold.

He probed the rock bonds that secured Dominic's wrists and ankles, manipulating the structure with imperceptible shifts, not removing the rings but stretching them until there was space between the rock and Dominic's skin. Only a close inspection would show there was room for Dominic to pull free when he needed to.

Evrain struggled to his feet. "Come on, you bastard. Let's finish this. You haven't beaten me yet," Evrain shouted into the wind and rain, his voice hoarse. He was sure the test wasn't yet over because there was one element left that hadn't yet been employed against him. Fire. He spared a second to wonder why his test was so much more severe than Gregory's. Someone had something against him that was certain.

"It was good of you to ease my way for the final part of the test." The dark figure at the edge of the hollow reappeared. "Time for you to face the dragon from the fairy tale, don't you think?"

Evrain shook his head. "What are you talking about? Dragons don't exist."

"It appears young warlocks today are severely lacking in imagination."

The ground beneath Evrain's feet trembled and he skidded sideways in the mud, fighting to keep his balance. A deep, menacing rumble came from the crevasse he had created and clouds of steam began to form. Grateful for the heat, Evrain attempted to relax his shoulders and regain some alertness. He peered into the crack, watching in fascinated horror as a fiery orange glow rose toward him.

"Magma? You have to be fucking kidding me." His examiner had to be an immensely powerful warlock to pull molten rock to the surface. He remembered Gregory telling him that the warlock chosen to test him would be given a boost to his power. This was a warlock on magical steroids. Despite the rising heat, Evrain shivered. Next to him, Dominic stirred and moaned but didn't fully awaken. "Fuck, not now. Dominic, love, if you can hear me, stay put. Don't move."

Evrain moved away, hoping to draw whatever was coming away from Dominic, who would be utterly helpless against it. An air cushion wasn't going to provide much protection against the heat of molten rock.

Magma welled to the surface of the crevasse then spilled over its edges, pooling in sluggish, crusted streams. As Evrain watched in horrified fascination, the pools joined, coalesced, then rose in a disturbing parody of a dragon, misshapen and deformed. It bore no resemblance to any mythical creature he'd seen in a childhood book of fairy tales, in a Disney movie or anywhere else for that matter. It was the stuff of nightmares, malevolent and intent on Evrain's destruction.

"Do something, you moron." Evrain drew on his deepest reserves, pulling the cold air from high above him down to surround the dragon, chilling its surface. The effort it took was immense and for a brief moment he thought it had worked as the dragon's 'skin' stiffened and blackened to a shell. But then glowing cracks appeared and the shell fell away. Evrain dodged a stream of fiery rocks by the scantest of margins. Cursing, he sought the remnants of hail in the atmosphere. If air didn't work, perhaps water would. Freezing liquid pounding against the dragon's shape produced hissing jets of boiling steam that scalded Evrain's skin. He twisted his hands into increasingly complex shapes, drawing on every lesson Gregory had ever drummed into him, to keep the ice frozen. The dragon sank toward the ground, just its eyes glowing red.

The pulse of power that shattered Evrain's defenses shook him to the bone. He let out a desperate sob as the dragon began to form once more, bigger and hotter than before. He had no idea what to do. The dragon was fashioned from the earth — any attempt to use that element was going to make the situation worse.

"*Fight fire with fire, love.*" Dominic's gentle voice filled Evrain's mind. He cast an urgent glance Dominic's way but his eyes were still closed. Relieved, Evrain though about his words. It seemed like madness, but fire was

Evrain's strength. He worked quickly, raising the temperature of the molten rock higher and higher, screaming his frustration, praying to any god that might be listening to give him a hand. He felt the bonds within the magma loosen and the outline of the monster blurred, losing definition. Evrain didn't dare stop—he poured his power into increasing the temperature until finally, the dragon exploded into a gaseous cloud, dissipating on the wind. Something inside Evrain's tortured body broke and this time he couldn't resist the darkness that crashed over him.

\* \* \* \*

"Am I dead?" Evrain regained consciousness with a jolt and a not inconsiderable amount of pain. "Hurts enough to be dead. Fuck."

"You're not dead." The amusement in Dominic's patient tone gave Evrain the will to crack an eyelid. "You look it, but you're breathing so I'm thinking funeral arrangements are premature, which is good because black doesn't suit me."

"Where's…"

"The tester?" Dominic blinked. "He dropped by, along with his partner. He had a few choice curse words to share about you. Apparently you gave him quite the headache. His partner was sweet though, and a tad more apologetic."

"He didn't hurt you?" Evrain heaved himself into a sitting position, glancing around in confusion. "Wait, where the hell am I? What happened to the cavern? How on earth did you get me back through those underground passages?"

"He said the illusion had been some of his best work… Killian, that is. The other warlock."

"Illusion my ass. There was a mine shaft, workings, then this huge hollow where a cave roof had fallen in. I climbed a fucking mountain to get to a usable entrance shaft. You were laid out on a slab like some sacrificial princess from a bad B-movie."

"Wow, it sounds impressive."

Evrain was not impressed by Dominic's admiration for the other warlock. He scowled. "He… I… Oh fuck it, I'll tell you later. Where are we?"

"Just inside the boundary fence to the mine workings. The car is over there." Dominic gestured over Evrain's head. "I woke up next to you about half an hour ago. I had the most peculiar dreams…well, nightmares I suppose. There was ice, thorns, a waterfall, a volcano? Not sure, it's all a bit hazy. Killian appeared, checked if I was okay, felt for your pulse…he said you may have over-extended yourself a little."

"He… I'm gonna kill him. Slowly. With a rusty tin opener to the balls."

"You can't. He left in a helicopter fifteen minutes ago, while you were still snoozing. He said, after forty years of testing warlocks from all over the planet, he'd never come across one with so much power, so young. He told me I had his sympathy."

"I was not snoozing! Whose side are you on?" Evrain cast a critical gaze over Dominic. He was disheveled but apparently not injured. Dark circles around his eyes and a few lines of tension betrayed how frightened he really was.

"Yours. Always yours." Dominic dropped to his knees next to Evrain then flung his arms around him.

He burst into desperate sobs. "I thought you were gone. Don't ever do that to me again."

Evrain held him close, absorbing his warmth. "I'm here. I'm fine. Never gonna leave you. Not ever. You're mine, remember." He hardly knew what he was saying, just that he had to give comfort to his shattered lover. "We need to get out of here. Do you think you can drive, because I don't think I can manage that?"

Dominic snuffled a damp confirmation into Evrain's neck. He pulled away with reluctance. "I'm pathetic. You're wet, cold and hurt and here I am acting like a child. I can't do anything for you here. Are we going back to the hotel?"

"Yes. I want to get off this island as quickly as possible. No offense to the people of Skye but it'll be a cold day in hell before I come here again."

"Can you make it to the car?"

Evrain wasn't sure he could stand but nothing was going to stop him leaving. He dragged himself to his feet, every muscle protesting. He gritted his teeth, refusing to upset Dominic by letting him know how much pain each and every movement caused. The short trip to the car was agonizing and by the time he slumped into the passenger seat, Evrain had to fight to hold on to consciousness. Dominic fussed over him, reclining the seat so he could stretch out, before getting behind the wheel. He turned the heat on full. "Sleep now. I'll wake you when we get back to the hotel."

"I'm fine."

"You are *not* fine. For once, I'm in charge, so do as I tell you, Evrain Brookes, or I'll... I'll..."

"You'll what?" Evrain liked this new, commanding side to Dominic.

"I'll withhold bedroom benefits for a week."

"Bedroom benefits?" Evrain snickered.

"No sex, Ev. Not unless you behave."

"Pretty sure that's gonna hurt you as much as me, love."

"Don't care... What is it you Brits say? No nookie. You need to rest. I've never seen skin quite that shade of gray before."

"Gray has never been my color." Evrain's words slurred. Sleep wasn't such a bad idea. "The test is over, right? No more nasty surprises?"

"It's over. It's safe to rest, sweetheart."

"'Kay." Evrain couldn't hold his eyelids up any longer. Even the bumpy track out of the mine workings couldn't keep him from sleep.

Dominic clung to the steering wheel much tighter than he needed to. He was angry, absolutely furious, that Evrain had been hurt. He wanted to hear every detail of the test he had been an unwilling part of. Evrain must be wondering why, and how, Dominic had disappeared from the hotel, but that could all wait. He wanted Evrain in a place where he could strip him bare and examine every wound, however small. He planned a long soak in the bath followed by a first aid session and a hot meal. It was a shame Killian couldn't have transported them back to the hotel using magic. The mundane function of driving seemed surreal somehow, but the winding road out of the Cuillins took concentration—it kept his mind from imploding. No doubt Evrain would have covered the distance quicker, but Dominic took extra care with the unfamiliar, wild terrain. He recognized the tension in his shoulders when he reached the Skye Bridge, groaning at his cracking joints when he rocked his head from side to side. He needed a massage in the worst way. Lying on a cold stone slab for Lord only knew how long hadn't helped, his back and hips ached horribly.

Crossing the bridge felt like an important milestone, placing the test in the past. It wasn't far back to Plockton and the hotel, but Dominic took his time, wanting to give Evrain some much needed rest before he had to wake him. It was strange to be the one in charge. Dominic was so used to submitting to Evrain, to letting him take the lead, that even having a modicum of control was alien. He didn't like it. He felt unsure and vulnerable without Evrain's steady, authoritative presence.

"I can do this." He ground the gears changing down and cursed before shifting more smoothly. "Foreign driving doesn't count. Why don't these people use automatics like the rest of the sane world?"

"Because we prefer to caress the engine into obedience rather than let it do its own thing." Evrain gave him a sleep-infused smile.

"I woke you! Sorry." Dominic blushed as he realized Evrain wasn't talking about the car. "We're almost back—just a few more minutes. Not sure how we're gonna get you inside without arousing a lot of curiosity, though. You look like a plane crash survivor or something."

"The room key is in the glove compartment. I didn't hand it in, so we wait for reception to be busy then walk past. We'll take the stairs rather than wait for the elevator, then we won't be trapped with other people. And, if anyone does ask, we say I took a tumble while we were out hiking."

"Can you manage the stairs?"

"That nap has worked wonders. Don't worry about me."

"You're such a liar." Dominic steered the car into a parking space as close to the hotel's door as he could get. "But I'll let you off until we get upstairs. Then I'm in charge."

Evrain licked his lips. "That sounds...intriguing."

"You're incorrigible."

"I'm the man that survived a warlock trial intact. I have a new appreciation for being not dead."

Dominic snorted. He turned off the ignition and relaxed in his seat. The silence was blissful.

"Let's go, gorgeous. We have a lot of catching up to do and I don't know about you, but I'm starving. I could eat an entire Aberdeen Angus."

"No!" Dominic had to protest. "They're the cute hairy orange ones, aren't they?"

"Yep, and very tasty they are too."

"Stop! I'm going to become a vegetarian. Promise me you won't order the cute cow."

"You are so soft-hearted." Evrain leaned across and planted a kiss on Dominic's cheek. "But fine. I enjoy a good mushroom risotto as much as the next man. Can we get inside now?"

"Oh! Yes." Dominic shook his head. He'd been debating food choices when Evrain was bleeding in the passenger seat. "I'm not doing a very good job, am I?"

"You're doing fine."

Dominic didn't believe him. He noted every cringe and wince as Evrain traversed the busy reception area. He limped ahead up the stairs and their luck held, not passing a soul on the way to their floor. Closing the door to their room behind them achieved sanctuary. The peace and quiet cleared Dominic's head and he swung into action. Taking care of his lover was something he *could* do.

# Chapter Seven

"Take your clothes off, Evrain. I'm going to run you a bath." When Evrain didn't move, Dominic frowned. He set the bath running then returned to help Evrain undress.

"Sorry. Everything hurts." Evrain stood placid as Dominic removed items of filthy, sodden, torn clothing.

"I'm not surprised. Sit on the edge of the bed."

Evrain plonked his bare ass on the edge of the mattress, which allowed Dominic to pull off boots, socks and pants. He grabbed a hotel robe, slinging it around Evrain's shaking shoulders to keep him warm while he attended to the bath. He was worried—he'd never known Evrain so quiet and still.

"I'm going to be fine, you know." Dominic spun around to find Evrain leaning against the doorframe. "I need sleep, that's all. I can see the cogs whirring in that brain of yours, so stop worrying. I'm not going to keel over, though I think you'll need to join me in the bath just in case I fall asleep and drown."

"Stop leering. You need to save your energy." Dominic hid a smile and swirled his hand through the water, checking the temperature. The soft impact of fabric against tile told Dominic that Evrain had dropped the robe. A touch to his hair brought him to his feet and he gasped. Large parts of Evrain's beautiful body were bruised, grazed or cut. He held his hands stiffly as if moving his fingers hurt. Skin that hadn't been covered by clothing was coated in a layer of muck. "In the water. Right now!"

With careful movements Evrain climbed into the tub. He lowered himself into the water with a happy sigh. "Feels great, but it'll be even better when you're in here with me."

It was pointless to argue that Evrain would be better off soaking alone. The tub was big enough for two with room to spare so Dominic stripped, leaving his clothes where they fell. He knelt in the water facing Evrain, the water reaching his waist, then lathered a sponge with creamy soap. With tender strokes he cleaned Evrain's battered body, working down from the shoulders. Every swipe seemed to reveal another cut or bruise.

"I want to know how you got every one of these," Dominic muttered as blood from a freshly opened cut stained the water.

"And I'll tell you." Evrain grabbed his wrist. "But now I want you to turn around and lean against me. I want your skin against mine." He parted his legs to make room. With some clumsy sploshing, Dominic managed to sit in the vacated space and lean his back against Evrain's chest.

"Tell me if I hurt you," he said, not resting his whole weight on Evrain's body.

In answer, Evrain wrapped his arms around Dominic's waist, pulling him closer. "Need to feel you." He trailed his fingers over Dominic's belly, moving lower until he could wrap his fist around Dominic's flaccid cock. "This is mine. You're mine. No one is ever going to separate us without my permission again." His fierce tone sent a shiver through Dominic's body.

"Okay."

"That's it? Just okay?"

"Not gonna argue with something I like the sound of. Life's way too short."

"Good." Evrain relaxed against the end of the bath as if Dominic's response had drained the tension from his body. "I wish we could stay like this forever."

"We'd both end up wrinkled as prunes."

"Then we should relocate to bed."

"Not until you've eaten. I need to wash your hair too, and we're sitting in icky water so a quick rinse is required."

"Slave driver." Evrain made no attempt to move.

"The quicker you're clean, the sooner we can be tucked beneath the covers." Evrain still had a firm hold of Dominic's cock and seemed to have no immediate intention of letting go. "Um, Ev…?"

"What?"

"I need my dick back."

"But I wanna keep it," Evrain whined, making Dominic chuckle.

"You're half asleep. You can have it back when we're in bed."

Evrain pouted but loosened his grip so that Dominic could deal with the shower head attached to the taps. He persuaded Evrain to his knees, pulled out the plug then shampooed and rinsed first Evrain's hair, then his own. By the time he was satisfied that Evrain was free of blood and grime and dry enough for bed, Evrain could hardly keep his eyes open.

"We don't have much in the way of first aid supplies," Dominic muttered. "Just a few bandages and some antiseptic cream. The wound on your upper arm is quite deep."

"Got stuck by a thorn," Evrain said. "Don't ask. Stick a plaster on it. I heal fast." He dressed in a soft T-shirt and shorts.

After dressing in similar attire, Dominic smoothed cream on all the open wounds he could find, covering any that still bled. He steered Evrain to an armchair and made sure he was comfortable before ordering room service. He didn't dare let him lie down before he'd had something nourishing to eat.

"Keep me awake," Evrain mumbled. "Tell me how they got you away from me last night."

Dominic settled on the floor between Evrain's legs. "Okay, though the more I think about it, the more idiotic I feel. I thought I was dreaming. I should have been more alert."

"Whatever happened wasn't your fault." Evrain twined his fingers into Dominic's hair. "Got it?"

Dominic rubbed his cheek against Evrain's thigh. "I was having this amazing dream where we made love. You wanted to take a walk along the loch, in the moonlight—it sounded romantic. You had a picnic blanket and this look in your eyes…"

"I am irresistible."

"And big-headed!"

"Go on."

"I knew it was a dream because one minute you were there in the room, the next you weren't. I could hear you calling from outside and I looked out of the window to see you standing on the shoreline. Um…you weren't wearing any clothes."

"Good to know what kind of fantasies you have."

"I had to be with you, so I crept out of the hotel. Everything was sprinkled with fairy dust—all sparkling and silver. The moon was huge, swollen. None of it seemed real. I thought I was going to wake up at any moment. You kept moving further away from me and I ran to keep up. My feet got wet in the shallows."

"I would never run away from you."

"Dream, remember?" Dominic sighed. "There was a sting on my neck. I remember thinking it was an odd time for a bee to be out and about. Things got a bit hazy from then on, but there was a helicopter, the rotor blades whipping spray from the water. Someone caught me as I fell. I thought it was you."

Evrain massaged Dominic's scalp in soothing motions.

"I don't remember anything clearly after that. The dream went on…something about fairy tales and dragons. You were there and you channeled again and again. It hurt and I tried to talk to you…I said…"

"Fight fire with fire."

"Yes! I don't know why that came into my head but I knew I had to let you know."

"You're the only reason I passed the test, love. I was on the verge of giving up…it wouldn't have occurred to me to use an element against itself."

There was a knock at the door. "That must be room service." Pulling his robe around him, Dominic admitted the waiter who placed a heavy tray on the table next to Evrain. Once he was gone, Dominic pulled the covers from the dishes. "I ordered comfort food. French onion soup and lamb stew." Aromatic scents wafted around the room.

"Not turning veggie just yet then?"

"Not tonight."

The warming meal had a soporific effect on both of them. Evrain's eyes were closing as soon as his fork clattered onto the plate. Leaving the empty dishes where they lay, Dominic locked the door before helping Evrain into bed. For a while he lay next to him, listening to him breathe. No longer tired, he was content to keep watch, his fingers intertwined with Evrain's. Though the test was over, Dominic couldn't quite convince himself that they were safe. If that meant a few sleepless hours, then so be it.

* * * *

After a dreamless night, Evrain awoke feeling refreshed and wondered for a few moments if he'd imagined the events of the last twenty-four hours. The aches and pains when he moved let him know he wasn't the victim of his own over-active imagination. He stifled a groan, not wishing to wake Dominic who was tucked close to his side, one arm flung across Evrain's waist. Dominic gave a cute snuffle, nosing into the crook of Evrain's arm. Evrain pushed a few strands of hair away from his face and Dominic's lashes fluttered. They were the same dark, burnished red as his hair, glinting with hints of copper fire.

"Good morning." Evrain leaned down to plant a soft kiss on Dominic's cheek.

"No."

"No?"

"I don't want it to be morning. I wanna stay here and cuddle." Dominic pouted, the jutting lower lip tempting Evrain to take a nip. He settled for shifting Dominic onto his back before sliding beneath the covers to find something even more irresistible.

"Fuck!" Dominic's hips jerked, pushing his cock to the back of Evrain's throat. Evrain chuckled around his mouthful then proceeded to draw an interesting selection of curse words from Dominic. Dominic tasted of herbs and home. His shaft was thick enough to make Evrain's jaw ache, but there was little he enjoyed more than bringing Dominic to a breath-holding precipice, only to push him back from the edge at the last possible moment. Doing the same thing whilst filling his ass was better, but this morning Evrain was happy to torment his lover with licks and swirls of his tongue.

"Stop torturing me, you sadist!"

Dominic's plea had nothing to do with Evrain's decision to bring him to completion. He wanted Dominic's seed in his mouth, something of him that no one else would ever have. Evrain sucked hard, compressing the head of Dominic's cock with his lips before plunging forward to take him deep to the back of his throat. He held still, enjoying the power of the moment before swallowing, wrenching a cry of release from Dominic's throat. Dominic's release coated Evrain's tongue, the taste familiar and deeply satisfying. Evrain hummed his pleasure, licking Dominic clean before re-emerging from beneath the sheets. Dominic looked shell-shocked, his eyes glazed. He made an unintelligible sound that Evrain took as pleasure. Feeling smug, he pulled Dominic over so that his head laid on Evrain's chest. Dominic wriggled downward but Evrain stopped him.

"That was for you."

"But…"

"No buts, I'm fine. I'll have my wicked way with you again later."

"Is that a promise?"

"Yes." Evrain stroked Dominic's back, working lower until he could grab a handful of ass. He let his fingers wander between warm cheeks, pushing between Dominic's thighs to tickle his balls. "I think we should show a face at breakfast—prove to the hotel staff that we're still alive and not up to anything nefarious." To mark the statement his stomach rumbled. "I need to call Gregory as well. Should have done that last night."

"I think you have a reasonable excuse, you were exhausted, and besides, I'll bet he's already heard the outcome of the test from one of his contacts. He seems to know everyone who's anyone in warlock circles."

"Hmm…I'm still glad we're on separate continents. I think I'm going to get an ear bashing of epic proportions."

"Why don't you call him while I take a quick shower, then I don't have to witness your humiliation. Give him and Coryn my love."

"Chicken." Evrain tracked Dominic to the bathroom, licking his lips at the delicious sight of a gently swaying ass.

"No, just sensible enough to know when hiding is the best option." Dominic disappeared into the bathroom, closing the door behind him with a decisive click.

Evrain debated following him to make good on his earlier promise but decided that delaying would just result in increasing Gregory's ire. He grabbed his phone, did a rough calculation of what the time would be in Oregon, then dialed anyway. Gregory picked up in seconds.

"Evrain."

Evrain swallowed. Gregory's stern voice wasn't fun. "Hi, Gregory."

"Good to know you're alive. Finally."

"Sorry?" Evrain held the handset away from his ear as Gregory let rip with a tirade about disrespectful young warlocks with no consideration for how worried their frail, infirm godparents might be. Evrain held back a snort at that statement. "Yes, sir." He decided that was the only safe response.

"That being said, well done, young man! I hear you had quite the rite of passage."

"Understatement of the millennium," Evrain muttered.

"What was that?"

"It was tough, to say the least."

"Killian was impressed, as much as that curmudgeonly old bastard ever is. He said he threw everything at you."

"It was Dominic who beat him, not me."

"False modesty. I don't doubt Dominic had a significant influence on the outcome, but you are the one with the power, Evrain. After that test, rumors about you will be circling the warlock community around the globe."

"Is that a good thing?"

"They'll think twice before messing with you, that's for sure. The test has confirmed what I already knew — that you're the most promising young warlock in generations. Of course, that doesn't mean you should get a swollen head. You have a long way to go with your training."

Evrain groaned. "You have to be kidding me. I thought this was a marker that I didn't need tuition anymore."

"Pah. Don't be ridiculous. You're still a baby, just out of diapers. However, that can wait until you return to the US. You and Dominic deserve a vacation. Have you contacted Lyssa yet?"

"Not yet." Evrain braced himself for another verbal spanking.

"Well, I suggest delaying for a while otherwise she and James will expect you to go straight there. I'll call her and lay the groundwork for why you can only make a brief stop. Take some time for the two of you first. You need to reconnect without the stress and trauma you've just been through. How are you feeling—and I don't mean the cuts and bruises I know you must have?"

"Drained. I don't think I'll be needing the bracelet for a while."

"You'll recover quicker than you think but I'd suggest you don't attempt to tap into your power for a few days at least."

"That won't be a problem." Just the thought of attempting to channel made Evrain yawn.

"Call me again when you're with the family. In the meantime, enjoy yourselves. All your expenses will be covered…within reason. Spoil Dominic."

"Thanks, Gregory, I will. I'll talk to you soon—you know I appreciate your support."

"This was all you, Evrain. You've turned into a fine young man…even if you do need to improve your communications skills." Gregory, always one to demand the final word, rang off before Evrain could think up a suitable retort. He flopped back against the pillows, rolling his eyes when Dominic peeked around the bathroom door.

"Is it safe to come out yet?"

Evrain examined the towel that barely covered Dominic's interesting parts and the droplets glistening on his chest. "Safe...no, I don't think you could call it safe out here. Drop that towel and I'll show you just how dangerous it is."

Dominic's eyes widened and color bloomed on his cheeks. He nibbled his lower lip. Evrain pushed the sheets down to expose his rigid erection. "Come here, love. Don't make me ask you again." Blinking, Dominic let the towel fall. "Breakfast can wait a little longer."

# Chapter Eight

It gave Evrain huge pleasure to show Dominic around the Highlands, especially the places he had loved as a child. Dominic wasn't ashamed to be a tourist, clambering over castle ruins, gazing wide-eyed at mountain scenery and spending hours on the shore of Loch Ness trying to spot the monster. They hiked for miles, indulged in home-cooked meals in small country inns and stayed in luxurious boutique hotels. The rich food was soon worked off with all the fresh air and exercise. They got wet more often than not, but Dominic declared Scotland suited a dramatic, stormy atmosphere — nothing could dampen his spirits and his boundless enthusiasm lifted Evrain's mood as he recovered from the ordeal of the testing. Cuts and bruises healed, but the psychological impact of what he had been through had left its mark. He didn't sleep well, often waking in the middle of the night, sweat-soaked from nightmares that almost always involved Dominic getting hurt. The subject of his dreams was always there to comfort him, reassure him and love him back to sleep—but Evrain found it hard to shake his fears. He and Dominic grew ever closer and Evrain found it impossible to imagine what life would be like without Dominic at his side.

With flights back to the States booked for the following day, they made their way to Evrain's childhood home for a final dinner. Gregory had done as he'd promised and paved their way with excuses about the trip being for business, not pleasure, and that Evrain had done his best to squeeze in enough time to visit the family. Evrain guessed Gregory had probably gotten short shrift from Evrain's mother, but he didn't care. Much as he loved his family, the time he and Dominic had spent alone together had been precious. They had been through a dangerous, traumatic ordeal and needed to heal in peace.

As Evrain parked the rental car outside his parents' looming Victorian house, he turned to Dominic. "You're looking a bit pale, sweetheart. Are you feeling all right?"

"Sure. Just a little nervous is all." Dominic fiddled with his collar. "Should I have worn a tie?"

"If you showed up in a manure sack they'd be delighted," Evrain said. "Honestly, you have nothing to worry about. It's one dinner. My mum will attempt to stuff enough food into you to last at least a week. My dad will bore you with history lectures about everywhere we visited and my sisters will probably try to convince you that I'm nowhere near good enough for you. Of course, they're right." He brushed a lock of hair away from Dominic's eyes, then kissed him. He was half considering turning the car around and heading for the hotel so that he could strip Dominic naked and do wicked things to him when there was a rap at the window, which made him jump out of his skin.

"Cut it out, you two. Mum says if you don't come inside in the next two minutes she'll be out here herself, and I don't think you want her to witness the two of you snogging, do you?"

"Charming as always, Jenna," Evrain yelled through the window. "One of my sisters," Evrain explained to Dominic, who was doing his best to disappear into his seat. "Time to face the inquisition, love."

Evrain clambered out of the car to be engulfed in hugs from both his younger sisters.

"Did you bring us presents?"

"We haven't been traveling around shopping for you, Julia." Evrain pushed them away to arm's-length so he could take a proper look. "Looking good, demon spawn." He tugged Jenna's hair and prodded Julia's shoulder. They both pounced on him, pummeling him into submission. "All right, all right, enough! You're scaring Dominic."

Dominic edged around the car, hands thrust deep in his pockets, head down, nibbling on his lower lip.

"Oh my Lord, big brother, where did you find this one? He's perfect." Jenna launched herself at Dominic, closely followed by her sister. Dominic had no choice but to open his arms for a hug. He mouthed 'help me' at Evrain, staring at him wild eyed from above the girls' heads. Before Evrain could do anything, Jenna and Julia took one of Dominic's hands each and towed him toward the house. Evrain fetched the bag of gifts from the back of the car then locked it and followed, chuckling.

When he reached the hall he found Dominic already shaking hands with his father. The girls' laughter could be heard coming from the direction of the kitchen, where they were no doubt regaling their mother with tales of Evrain's arrival and his misbehavior in the car.

"Hello, son." James Brookes was a shade under Evrain's height, but his broad shoulders made him seem taller somehow.

"Dad. Great to see you." Evrain walked into an easy hug. His dad had never been the kind of man to shy away from affection.

"You look pale, tired. I hope Gregory isn't working you too hard?"

"Not at all," Evrain said. "I love the job at ThInk and the opportunity to come over here was brilliant. I'm glad we managed to fit in a visit."

"If you hadn't, your mother would have hunted you down and subjected you to the kind of embarrassment that would go down in family history. Hello, Dominic, it's nice to finally meet you in person. Shout if you need somewhere quiet to hide—this place is a zoo at the best of times. You'd better get yourselves into the kitchen or I'll be accused of keeping you to myself. Go say hello, then join me in the lounge for a drink."

Evrain took Dominic's hand and led him to the back of the house and the heart of the Brookes' home, the kitchen. His mother was putting the finishing touches to an enormous pie while the girls had been put to work at the sink, washing and drying a mountain of dishes. Evrain took a long look at his mum. There was flour on her chin and in her hair. She hadn't changed a bit, still looking ten years younger than her actual age.

"Hey, Mum, this is Dominic."

Lyssa Brookes looked up with a smile. "Here you both are at last." She gave Evrain a hug and a kiss on the cheek. "And, Dominic, I've seen pictures of course, but I never imagined..." She drew Dominic into her arms. "I'm so glad you're here."

Evrain suspected that his mum was close to tears—her eyes were certainly brighter than usual. "Dad said there would be drinks in the lounge, so we'll leave you to it, unless there's anything we can do?"

"Go and relax," Lyssa said. "There will be time enough over dinner for me to ask all the questions I want to ask of both of you. A weekly phone call just isn't enough. The first course is ready so tell your father to go on through to the dining room, you can take your drinks in there. Once he gets settled in that sofa it takes a crane to get him out again."

Evrain nodded, glaring at his sisters, who were giggling and grabbing quick looks at Dominic over their shoulders. He guided Dominic back to the lounge where his father was pouring a deep red wine into the best lead crystal goblets. Evrain seized the one he was offered and took a long swallow. "Very nice. Has Mum broken out the best china too?"

"You know your mum—she just wants to make a good impression on your young man. I'm afraid, Dominic, that you are the main attraction tonight. Much as we love having Evrain home, you've got novelty value."

"Oh God." Dominic took several sips of his wine. "I won't know what to say."

"Don't worry, son, you can sit between me and Evrain. We'll protect you from the coven."

Evrain gripped Dominic's free hand. "Don't panic, not that kind of coven," he whispered.

A large, hairy dog of indeterminate breed barreled into the room. His paws almost reached James' shoulders when he jumped up, tongue lolling.

"Since when did you get a dog?" Evrain asked.

"Your mum started volunteering at the shelter. This guy had been there a while, probably because he eats as much as a small family, and of course she couldn't resist him. His name is Bunsen and he's... Actually I'm not sure what he is. I think there's some St. Bernard in him, maybe Collie and perhaps a bit of German Shepherd. Who knows? He's interesting and he loves everybody, even the postman. He also watches the History Channel with me without complaining."

Dominic was already on his knees, petting Bunsen. "We've been thinking of getting a dog too," he said. "I work from home most of the time now and there's plenty of space for a dog to run around." Bunsen put an enormous paw on Dominic's thigh. "We have to find one that likes cats, though."

"This one tries to make friends with anything that moves. Cats, squirrels, muntjac... Even the yappy little terrier that lives at the other end of the village. Bunsen is twenty times bigger than her but he thinks they're soulmates."

Dominic got to his feet, brushing hair from his pants.

"Sorry about that," James said. "I should have said that he molts everywhere. We're going to have to invest in an industrial vacuum cleaner."

"Mum said we should go through to the dining room," Evrain said.

"Then that's what we must do." His dad grinned, grabbing the half-empty wine bottle. "I've already put a couple more bottles on the table."

"Don't let me get too carried away," Evrain said. "I'm driving."

"You could always stay here, you know."

"We have an early flight and our hotel's right by the airport. Otherwise we would have done."

"Then you'll have to try the elderflower cordial your mother's made this year. It's much less poisonous than it usually is." James rolled his eyes and Dominic laughed. Evrain was glad to see him relaxing.

Once the meal was served and everyone was eating and talking at once, Dominic was much more at ease. He answered questions with good humor, brushing off compliments from Jenna and Julia who seemed to think everything about him was perfect though they couldn't understand how he had ended up with their reprobate of a brother.

Evrain was so full by the time they were done, he couldn't have fit in another mouthful. They moved back to the lounge for coffee, positioning themselves to accommodate Bunsen, who had sprawled across the floor and seemed to have no intention of moving for anyone.

"He's certainly made himself at home, hasn't he?" Evrain said.

"Isn't he gorgeous?" His mum leaned forward to pet Bunsen's glossy head. "He ended up at the shelter because his elderly owner passed away. The old man left provision for him in his will, would you believe? We've donated the money to the shelter, of course."

Bunsen opened one eye, as if understanding that he was the subject of the conversation.

"I'm intending to take semi-retirement from the university next year," James said. "I'm going to get down to writing the book I've been talking about for years and lecture three days a week."

"What's the book about?" Dominic asked.

Everyone else in the room groaned. "Ignore them," James said. "Bunch of Philistines, the lot of them. It's a history of the ancient kings of Scotland. Absolutely fascinating but quite difficult to research."

"Don't get him started," Lyssa said. "I've no doubt the book will eventually get written, but James has been talking about it for so long, and so often, that we'd all like him to lock himself in his study and get on with it." She gave her husband's knee an affectionate pat.

"And believe me, in a house full of women that is not going to be a problem." James' comical expression made Evrain snort into his wine as a chorus of indignant comments came from around the room.

The banter continued late into the evening. The girls eventually disappeared to bed after insisting on pictures with Dominic so that they could show their friends. Evrain sat back in his chair, cradling a mug of cocoa.

"How have you really been?" Lyssa asked. "Gregory told us what he could a while after you were born, and with Mum being the way she was, we're not completely ignorant about how *different* you are, sweetheart."

Evrain guessed she made the statement to reassure Dominic. "Gregory's looking after me," Evrain said. "I miss Gran, though."

"Her death was a shock to all of us," Lyssa said. "I hate that whoever did it has never been officially caught. But Gregory has assured me that the person responsible paid an appropriate price."

"He did and, if it's any reassurance, she loved the life she'd built at Hornbeam Cottage."

"She was right to give it to the two of you," Lyssa said. "It's clear as day that you were meant to be together." She sipped her wine then gave a sly smile.

"Mum... Don't." Evrain put all the warning he could muster into his expression.

"So when am I going to be able to plan a wedding?"

"You had to go there, didn't you? Couldn't stop yourself." James laughed, shrugging his shoulders when Evrain looked to him for help.

"Don't look at me, son. When you've been married as long as we have, you'll know which battles are worth fighting and those where it's best to offer unconditional surrender."

"We're just enjoying being together at the moment," Evrain said, reaching for Dominic's hand. Dominic squeezed his fingers.

"Well, don't make me wait too long. I know you don't have much in the way of your own relations, Dominic, but we are your family now and we just want the two of you to be happy. And married."

"Mum!" Evrain protested. "I swear if you don't stop, we'll run away to Vegas."

"You're not too old for a spanking, you know," Lyssa said, wagging a finger at Evrain.

Dominic snorted with laughter. Evrain scowled and began to plot all the ways he would get his own back. His dad gave him a knowing look, but said nothing. Bunsen snuffled and rolled onto his back, inviting tummy rubs. Dominic obliged and Evrain was content to watch his lover lavish affection on another male.

"Next time, you must come for a longer visit," James said.

"We will," Evrain replied, meaning what he said. Recent events had made a lot of things clearer in his mind. Dominic's and his family's love would never be taken for granted. Life was far too short.

# Chapter Nine

"Have you finished babying those plants yet?" Evrain, hands on hips, gave Dominic an impatient glare. "We've been away ten days, not ten weeks, and I think Coryn lavished more love and attention on them than he has on Gregory while they've been staying here."

Dominic fingered the velvet leaves of a young sage. "Hush, they'll hear you. Can you...you know?" He waggled his fingers. "Please."

Evrain couldn't resist the appeal in Dominic's eyes. Sighing he extended his senses into the earth, channeling carefully. He detected warm fertile soil, vibrant life in tangled roots and a multitude of small creatures. He warmed some cold patches and encouraged moisture into a dry section of ground, sensing Dominic's happiness through their bond as he worked. "Every earthworm in a five-mile radius is heading this way and you have the healthiest crop of plants in the state and it has very little to do with me."

"I missed them. That's stupid isn't it?" Dominic, on his knees, dug his fingers into the soil.

Evrain hated the word 'adorable' but that's exactly what Dominic was. It was an unavoidable fact that his lover was cute, gorgeous *and* adorable.

Tail held aloft, Shadow sashayed through the rows of herbs, waggling her ass. She put her front paws on Dominic's thigh then head-butted him until he stroked her.

"Hey, Shadow, bet you missed us, didn't you?" She gave him a disdainful look but climbed onto his lap nonetheless. "I'm not staying here, you know." Shadow kneaded Dominic's thighs for a full minute before jumping off to disappear into the bushes at the side of the garden. "Do you think that means I'm forgiven?" Dominic asked.

"Not even close. We're both going to need thigh protectors for the next few days at least." Evrain extended a hand. "And you're not being stupid, you're being you. However, we now have the cottage to ourselves and I think we should take advantage, don't you? I love Gregory and Coryn but between them, my family and traveling, I'm missing my alone time with you." Dominic accepted the hand and Evrain hauled him to his feet.

"You've been even more possessive than usual the last few days. No one's taking me away from you again, love."

Evrain drew him close. "It's a Neanderthal imperative. I have to claim you a few times to make sure all the surrounding cave dwellers know who you belong to." He tugged Dominic toward the house.

"I'm sure our neighbors would be delighted to know you think of them as prehistoric rivals."

"I'd rather not think of them at all. Biff Sawrey at The Gables gives me the evil eye every time I see him."

"You're imagining things. He has a bit of a squint, that's all." Dominic chuckled. "And he spends most of the year at his daughter's place in the Hamptons, so you have nothing to worry about."

"I'm not worried. Big bad warlock, remember?"

"Not so much at the moment."

"No, that's true." Evrain pushed his way into the cottage, latching the door behind them.

"How *are* you feeling? Is it getting better?"

"I won't be creating earthquakes any time soon." Evrain sighed. "Sorry, I don't mean to be glib." He ran a hand through his hair, leaving it sticking up in random tufts. "I'm still weak. The test drained everything I have. Gregory said that's deliberate, that I need to experience vulnerability. Once you understand the power and how to use it, there's a tendency to assume that you can't be hurt and that's not the case. I can feel it inside me. It hasn't gone away. It's like the tide has gone out and I'm waiting for it to come back in again." He pulled Dominic close so that they were pressed together, chest to groin. "The rest of me is in perfect working order though." He made sure Dominic could feel his erection.

"Apparently." Dominic's smile lit his eyes.

Evrain attempted to maneuver Dominic toward the stairs but met with some resistance.

"Can we...I mean, I'd like to talk for a bit, if that's okay?"

"Of course we can." Evrain's frustration was tempered by the appeal in Dominic's tone. "Shall I light a fire? It's getting a bit chilly."

"That sounds nice." Dominic chewed on his lower lip and Evrain wanted nothing more than to do violence to whatever was causing Dominic such anxiety. The grate was already laid with logs and kindling so it didn't take Evrain long to get a blaze going, even though he did use boring human means to do it. He stacked some more logs to make sure it would burn for a good while then took the armchair to one side of the hearth, patting his lap.

"Come here, love." To his relief, Dominic didn't hesitate. He clambered onto Evrain's lap and snuggled close.

"Sorry."

"What for?"

"Being so…pathetic."

"Honey, it's a miracle you're not a complete basket case after what you've been through. You're the strongest person I know."

"Do you think your family liked me? The warlock test was nothing compared to meeting them for the first time."

"You're kidding, right? If my mum had her way you'd never have been allowed out of the country. I think she was planning to confiscate your passport. You had her wound around your green little finger five minutes after walking through the door. Dad got out the photograph albums, for fuck's sake. Now that was truly humiliating."

"You were a very cute baby."

"I was naked ninety percent of the time. There should be a law against baby bath pictures. Dad was calling you son…I seriously think I've been replaced in his affections."

"That's 'cause I'm not a precocious brat. He told me so."

"And my sisters. Jesus."

"They were very sweet."

"Saccharine has nothing on them, mooning over your hair, your eyes, how much of a gentleman you are, how you could have done so much better than me."

"You're their big brother. They have to tease you — it's the law."

"If I had a pound for every hint my mother dropped about wedding plans, I'd be a rich man. They threatened to come visit, too. I thought moving an entire continent away would earn me some peace but no. The whole clan will be showing up on the doorstep before we know it."

"I never got to see you in your kilt, though." Dominic stroked Evrain's cheek.

"If you tell me what's really bothering you, I might oblige and put it on."

"It's just…well…do you think we'll have the chance to live normal lives for a while?"

"That would be nice. I could handle a bit of domestic bliss and God knows I need to put some time in at my job. They must think I'm a complete flake."

"You're the most talented artist they have working there. They're lucky to have you."

"Even so, I don't like letting them down by disappearing all the time. I know Gregory has influence and covers my behind, but my boss must be mightily pissed off. I shouldn't be hiding behind the fact that my godfather owns shares in the company."

"It's not like you haven't had good reasons for the time off you've taken. You weren't sunning yourself on a tropical beach. Between dealing with Symeon Malus, fighting off a coven of witches and facing the test, you should be taking a longer break, not worrying about how much time you spend at the office." Dominic's voice got more strident. "I just want to grow my herbs."

"And I want that for you. Very much." Evrain wrapped his arms around Dominic's shaking body.

"I sense a 'but' coming."

"What's the saying...with great power comes great responsibility. Where does that come from?"

"From some utter idiot."

"Maybe, but I have to admit that I like knowing there's a purpose behind us being the way we are. Warlocks I mean. Things kind of fell into place in my head when Gregory told me about our history. The test was horrific but I get why it's necessary. There's no way of knowing whether we'll ever be needed to help avert some great catastrophe, but we need to be ready. I have to train and do what Gregory tells me to, much as that gives me a migraine to think about, and that means you have to train too. Coryn hardly feels any pain when Gregory channels through him. I want it to be the same for us. I hate knowing I hurt you every time I focus my power."

"I accept it, you know I do. Coryn said it was time that helped ease things for him and he and Gregory have been together a very long time."

"But we have an exceptionally strong bond. When you were taken in Scotland, being apart was unbearable, a physical pain. I need to know where you are all the time and if that makes me a possessive, controlling bastard, so be it."

Dominic chuckled. He fiddled with the pendant resting against his chest. "You're always with me, taking care of me. It's selfish, but I don't want you being a hero too soon. I want to redecorate the bathroom, shop for new bedding, eat out every now and again. Get a dog."

"Oh, Shadow is going to love you."

"That wasn't a no."

"When have I ever been able to say no to you? And besides, I love dogs. What kind do you want?"

"Something dumb and loveable. A mutt. There's a rescue shelter not too far away."

"You've been putting some thought into this." Evrain wasn't sure whether he should be upset that Dominic hadn't confided in him sooner, but when had there been time? Their life together so far had been a whirlwind of drama and adventure. "We should get a dog with big teeth. Something that can protect you when I'm not there."

"I want a pet, not a guard dog! Wait, you're yanking my chain, aren't you?"

Evrain shrugged. "Maybe, maybe not."

"Sometimes I think I should be the one spanking you."

"Gregory might agree but that's never going to happen." Evrain could feel the beat of Dominic's heart against his chest, strong and true. "I love you, you know."

"I know." Dominic sighed. "I like this. When it's quiet and just the two of us with nothing to worry about. No monsters at the door."

Evrain gave the fire a mental nudge and the flames climbed a little higher.

"Shouldn't you be conserving your strength?"

"Apparently not. According to Gregory I'll recover quicker if I keep in practice, within reason. I shouldn't need to vent for a while, or wear the gold bracelet.

Though he thinks I might need another one once I'm back to full power. I should get you cuffs to match, ones that can be linked together."

"The kink runs deep in this one." Dominic attempted a Yoda impression.

"It does and you love it." Evrain lifted Dominic onto his feet. "And on that note, enough with the talking. I feel the need for physical activity. The exercise will do us both good after being cramped in cars and planes."

"First-class travel isn't that much of a chore." This time it was Dominic who tugged Evrain toward the stairs. "But I am a little stiff." He grinned. Evrain threw him over his shoulder in a fireman's lift then took the stairs at a run. By the time he hoisted Dominic onto the bed, they were both in fits of giggles. When Evrain managed to catch his breath, he affected a much sterner look.

"I'm going to strip you, cuff you to the bed then make long, slow love to you."

"Sounds perfect." Dominic leaned in for a kiss.

Evrain probed the warmth of Dominic's mouth while fumbling with his shirt buttons. He pushed the annoying fabric away then stood back to get a better view of Dominic's well-defined chest. "You're gorgeous." He pinched a nipple, twisting the nub of flesh until Dominic squeaked. "I love how sensitive you are." He smoothed Dominic's hair away from his shoulder so that he could taste his neck.

"Are you reliving Hallowe'en?" Dominic asked. "Gonna sink your fangs into my neck?"

"You do taste good enough to eat, but no." He nibbled on a soft earlobe. "I'm too impatient. Fetch the cuffs from the dresser."

The leather cuffs Dominic retrieved were soft from use. Evrain buckled them in place then had Dominic lie on his back on the bed. He used the linking chain to fasten the cuffs to the headboard, leaving Dominic with his arms stretched above his head.

"Perfect." Evrain went to work divesting Dominic of his socks, pants and underwear. "Not too cold?"

"Not at all. Think I'm on fire." Dominic wiggled his toes. "The anticipation is killing me, Ev."

"Then I won't make you wait." Any plans Evrain had for a drawn-out scene went out the window as Evrain admired taut muscles and smooth skin. His need to get inside his soul mate was all-consuming. He stripped with rapid efficiency, leaving his clothes where they fell. He made sure there was a jar of lube within reach and clambered onto the bed. Dominic was smiling, amusement apparent in his eyes.

"You're laughing at me," Evrain growled.

"Just happy that you're so eager."

Evrain grunted. "Spread your legs and bend your knees." He shoved a pillow under Dominic's ass.

"Charmer."

Evrain parted Dominic's cheeks and set to with his tongue, ensuring that the only sounds Dominic was capable of making were whimpers and squeals. He plunged his tongue into Dominic's hole again and again. Dominic clawed at the sheets. The tip of his cock gleamed with pre-cum. When Evrain was certain Dominic was about to come, he sat back.

"Hey!" Dominic glared at him, his eyes glazed. "Evil man."

"Oh hush. I've got you." Evrain slicked his cock with lube. "Just making sure you're nicely revved up and ready for me." After hefting Dominic's calves onto his shoulders he pressed into him, stilling once he was fully seated. He gazed into Dominic's eyes. "Now I have you where I want you."

"You always do."

"I love you." Evrain moved slowly at first, then quicker, monitoring Dominic's expressions as he gasped with pleasure. The first tingles of an impending orgasm circled the base of Evrain's spine. He sped up, pushing deep into Dominic's body. Dominic dropped one leg to the bed and twisted sideways, the new position giving Evrain a new angle to explore. He slowed again and Dominic growled.

"If I weren't tied to the headboard..."

Evrain chuckled but obliged and moved faster. He gripped Dominic's shaft, applying some friction and they came together, shouting each other's names in tandem. There was no need for words. Evrain released the chain between Dominic's cuffs, freeing him from the headboard, then joined them again. He gathered Dominic into his arms, sealing their lips together. They stayed that way for a long time.

Later, Evrain lay on his back, one arm thrown above his head, the other around Dominic. Most of the bedding had ended up on the floor in an untidy heap but one sheet remained tangled around his calves. The chain linking Dominic's wrist cuffs clinked, the sound sending a miniature bolt of lightning to Evrain's cock. "The cuffs will stay on for the night," he stated. "Gonna lock up your dick too."

Dominic raised his head. "You waited until I was too exhausted to fight back to tell me that, didn't you?"

"Would you say no if you weren't a puddle of goo?" There was no way Evrain would ever do anything to Dominic without his consent.

"I'm surprised you've waited this long. You've been threatening me with chastity for ages." Dominic hid his face against Evrain's chest. "The idea is kinda hot and I can't believe I'm admitting that."

Evrain's pulse sped up. He'd thought this might be a step too far for Dominic but the idea of holding the key to a device that imprisoned Dominic's pretty dick was a huge turn-on for Evrain. He wriggled out from beneath Dominic, clambered out of bed and went to the dresser. The package in his underwear drawer had been there a while. He took it out, leaving the box in the drawer, then went back to bed. Dominic had propped himself against the pillows, bound hands resting on his lap.

"Here, take a look." Evrain handed over the bespoke device. "It's made from palladium, which won't rust, or corrode."

"And is a natural metal so you can manipulate it," Dominic commented, his tone wry.

"I don't know what you mean," Evrain said, affecting innocence.

"There's nowhere for a padlock on this, Evrain, I'm not stupid." Dominic turned the metal over in his hands. "You're going to use your power to lock it, aren't you?"

"What's the use of having warlock abilities if I don't use them for interesting things?" He took the device back. "Lie down. Put your hands over your head."

Grumbling under his breath, Dominic did as he'd been told.

"Spread your legs nice and wide."

Evrain fitted the metal tube around Dominic's shaft. Metal strips separated his balls and encircled them at the base, making an attractive display. Twisting his fingers into a complex shape, Evrain connected with the earth element and coaxed it to do his bidding, contracting the metal until it was a snug fit, sealed shut. The hole in the end would allow Dominic to use the bathroom or Evrain to insert a sound, another idea he'd been playing with. He sat back to admire his handiwork. "Fuck, that looks hot. How does it feel? Not too tight?"

"It's a perfect fit. Heavy. Constricting."

"Good." Evrain jacked his emerging erection a few times until he was fully hard. He lifted Dominic's calves so that they rested on his shoulders. "Leave your hands where they are." Dominic was still well-lubricated. Evrain's cock slid into his body with ease, the slick heat welcoming. He bent Dominic back, pressing deep. "How does it feel, me taking you like this when you have no hope of coming?"

"No need to sound so gleeful." Dominic panted in time with Evrain's thrusts. Evrain silenced him with a kiss, punishing his lips.

"Be more respectful to the man who owns your body." He jacked his hips harder, digging his fingers into Dominic's hips.

"Sir!" Dominic screamed the word just as Evrain climaxed, pumping his seed deep into Dominic's body. "Please...please..."

Evrain drew in several long breaths, allowing the final ripples of his orgasm to roll over him. He withdrew with care, patting Dominic's ass before lowering his legs to the bed. "If you're good, I might let you come in the morning."

Dominic glared.

"Now, now, don't look at me like that." Evrain pushed Dominic's legs apart to stroke the taut skin of his balls. Dominic squirmed and tried to roll away. "I think I'll tie you to the bed and play a while longer."

Dominic's eyes widened.

"A gag would look good on you too." He smiled at Dominic's moan.

"Power-crazed warlock."

"That didn't sound like an objection."

"It wasn't." Dominic blinked, long lashes fluttering.

"I am a very lucky man." Evrain contemplated which plug to use to lock his seed inside his lover's body. *Something thick and ridged.*

"What are you smiling about?" Dominic asked. "Or do I not want to know?"

"Probably best you don't. You'll find out soon enough." He planted a kiss on Dominic's thigh then licked all the way to his groin. "Trust me, I'm a warlock."

# Chapter Ten

"It's so good to feel normal. I can't believe we're celebrating Hallowe'en like everybody else. Are you sure you don't mind doing this on your birthday?"

"I don't mind at all. It will be fun and besides, the kids will be gone early and I'll have you to myself for the rest of the evening."

"Do you think anyone will call?" Dominic finished putting the final touches to the carved pumpkin he intended to put outside the front door. He had the perfect white candle to put inside it.

"If they don't, we're going to be overdosing on candy for the rest of the year." Evrain shook the bucket he had just filled with candy, lollipops, miniature chocolate bars and some boxes of raisins for those kids with a healthier mindset. "You did a great job decorating. I'm sorry I wasn't around to help."

"I handed over my final gardening customers this morning. No more mowing lawns or trimming borders, I can concentrate on the herb business full-time. Not being tied to appointment times means I can be flexible when it comes to things like hanging skeletons and constructing giant spider webs."

"Finding Jordan and his brother was a godsend. I know you're going to miss some of your customers though."

"Some of them have been with me since I started up, but I've heard nothing but good feedback about Jordan and Tom. They're just starting out and it felt good to give them a helping hand with a readymade client list. I wish there had been someone around to do the same for me — I wouldn't have made so many mistakes when I was looking for customers. I also have invites back for afternoon tea, drinks, use of the pool... If I accepted them all I wouldn't get any work done at all."

"They all loved you. Not as much as I do of course."

Dominic gazed into Evrain's sparkling green eyes. "No one could ever love me as much as you do or as much as I love you." He extended his hand, sticky with pumpkin juice. Evrain ignored the mess and gave it a squeeze. "This is way too sappy. Are you done with that thing? I want to turn the lights on now it's dark and I still need to get changed into my costume."

"Me too. Let me wash up. I want to take a picture of the finished effect." It only took a minute or two to rinse his hands in the sink, grab his camera then head outside to join Evrain, who had lit the candles inside the latest pumpkin and several others that Dominic had made earlier. He'd also fixed up strings of fairy lights in the shape of ghosts, and some Chinese lanterns in red and orange. Everything was powered by miniature battery packs as they had no outside socket. Evrain made his way around to turn everything on.

"It all looks fantastic," Evrain said, admiring the tableau. "That massive rubber spider is going to give me nightmares, let alone the kids."

"It does look good. The lights make all the difference. It's good that it's a clear, dry night too."

Evrain slung an arm around Dominic's shoulders and squeezed. "We have time to share a shower before the kiddies arrive, don't we?"

"Not the kind of shower I know you're thinking about." Dominic gave him a quick kiss on the cheek.

"Killjoy. Fine, I'll be good but you have to promise me one thing."

"All right, I'll bite. What do you want?"

"You to stay in costume for the rest of the evening." Evrain had a wicked glint in his eye.

"Okay. If it'll make you happy." Dominic's cheeks heated and he was glad of the concealing darkness because Evrain always teased him when he blushed.

"In that case, I'll go first."

Evrain went inside but Dominic stayed where he was, wanting to enjoy the night air for a while. There was a slight scent of wood smoke coming from somewhere nearby and Dominic guessed that someone further up the street had a bonfire going. When he'd driven home at lunchtime he'd idled in the van, checking out all the decorations around the area. Some people had really gone to town and made a huge effort. He hoped the dark path from the end of the village to the cottage wouldn't put the kids off. He'd let some of the neighbors know that he and Evrain would be welcoming trick-or-treaters that night and couldn't wait to see the fancy dress costumes and excited faces. He'd even stuck a few solar lights along the path to make it less intimidating.

Pressure against his calves told him that he had a visitor. "Hi, Shadow, I hope you answer the door with us later. A black cat will be the perfect accessory tonight, you know."

Shadow meowed as if she'd understood every word. Dominic suspected that she did. She lifted a paw and gave it a few dainty licks. Rumbling purrs followed. "Come on inside and I'll give you your supper." With a last look at the decorations, Dominic went into the cottage. He opened a fresh can of tuna, spooning the contents into Shadow's empty bowl before placing it on the floor. She had her face in the food before the bowl reached the ground.

"You're a bottomless food pit." Dominic gave her a stroke, which she ignored.

"Bathroom's free," Evrain yelled from the top of the stairs. Dominic smiled. When he got to the bathroom he found Evrain standing outside it wearing nothing but a smile and jacking his cock with lazy motions.

"Just wanted you to see what you're missing."

Dominic licked his lips. Evrain smelled of the woods after a rainstorm, his skin was flushed from the heat of the shower and a few stray drops of water rolled down his chest. Dominic dropped to his knees. Evrain grabbed his hair and held tight as Dominic took his hot, rigid shaft into his mouth.

"Keep still. I'm gonna fuck your mouth."

Much as he enjoyed sucking Evrain's cock, Dominic loved it even more when Evrain took control. He didn't resist Evrain's hold but focused on giving Evrain as much pleasure as he could. He knew the spot under the head of Evrain's dick that drove him wild if he tongued it. The gentlest scrape of his teeth achieved grunts of pleasure and if he fondled Evrain's balls in time with sucking him, Evrain lost it completely. Dominic tried the latter then kept as still as he could while Evrain used his mouth, coming in hot salty bursts with a shout of delight.

Evrain leaned against the wall, dragging in gasps of air while Dominic staggered to his feet.

"That was… That was… I have no idea what that was other than bloody brilliant. Happy birthday to me!"

Dominic gave him a kiss, transferring the taste of Evrain's seed into his lover's mouth. "You are incorrigible and we're going to be late." He ran for the bathroom before Evrain could get any other ideas, slamming the door behind him. He stripped then got beneath the spray, hard cock already in hand.

"Jesus, Evrain, you're going to kill me." He jacked himself hard, already close to the edge. It didn't take long and he came with a shudder, eyes squeezed shut. When he regained enough composure to wash, he sluiced himself with shampoo and shower gel, taking the minimum amount of time possible. In his hurry, he almost tripped climbing over the side of the bath as he reached for a towel with water in his eyes. He caught himself just in time, thankful that the towel rail was well fixed to the wall. He dried off then strolled naked to the bedroom, toweling his hair as he went.

Evrain was already dressed in his vampire costume, the long cloak swirling around his knees. He had on a black shirt and leather trousers and had lightened his skin with white face paint. The final touches were a set of false fangs, one painted with a drop of blood on its tip, and a set of red contact lenses.

"There's no way I'm going to let you open the door looking like that," Dominic said. "All the neighborhood moms will be after you."

"The only person I want to sink these fangs into is you, love. You have nothing to worry about." Evrain did a little twirl. "I do quite like the costume though." He reached out to give Dominic's ass a slap but Dominic skipped out of reach.

"Oh no you don't, I have to get dressed too." He threw his towel over the back of a chair. His outfit was hanging in the wardrobe but he pulled on underwear first, choosing a clingy pair of shorts that elicited a couple of inappropriate comments from Evrain.

"Go downstairs, or I'll never get ready. You're a bad influence."

With a laugh, Evrain left the room. Dominic shook his head as his mischievous lover stomped down the stairs. He laid the costume Evrain had chosen on the bed, eyeing the deep red satin pants and thigh-high boots. He couldn't imagine that any genuine pirate would have worn such an outfit but Evrain had spotted it in the store and loved it. Dominic didn't mind the frilly shirt with its long sleeves and lace cuffs and the thigh-length waistcoat he wore over it would conceal how tight the trousers were. Because his hair was long he didn't bother with a wig, just tied it back with a black ribbon, perching the tricorn hat on his head. He applied a little makeup, outlining his eyes and sketching a fake scar down his cheek for effect. Content with the overall look, he went downstairs to join Evrain who was stirring something on the stove.

"That smells really good."

"It's mulled cider. One of Gran's recipes, so I raided your spice jars. And, by the way, you should wear thigh boots a lot more often."

Dominic ignored the comment and Evrain's leer. He leaned over the pan and took a deep breath, trying to detect the mixture of spices Evrain had used. "I can definitely smell cloves, nutmeg and cinnamon. There's orange juice in there and something else... Vanilla."

"Very good, but you've missed something." Evrain stirred a bit more and steam rose from the mixture.

"Hmm, I'm not sure." Dominic took a deep breath and caught a hint of aniseed. "Star anise!"

"That's right. Ten out of ten. I thought we could have this with the snacks you made, by the fire, while we wait for anyone to arrive."

"Sounds good. I'll deal with the food."

Earlier that day Dominic had made cheese straws, smoked salmon blinis and tiny bites of Melba toast with mushroom pâté. There was garlic bread to heat up in the oven as accompaniment to some soup for later on. He'd only just finished laying things out on the low table near the fire when there was a knock on the door. With Shadow weaving between his legs, he grabbed the candy bucket and went to open it.

"Oh look, Momma, it's a pirate!" The small child who spoke couldn't have been more than four years old and was wearing a sheet with holes cut out for the eyes. Dominic tried not to laugh. Two adults stood a little way down the path and one of them gave him a wave. He recognized Annie from the shop in the town, which meant the little boy was her youngest, Toby. Toby was accompanied by a Ninja Turtle and a fireman. They all dug their hands into the candy bucket and carefully extracted one item each.

"Go on, take another one each," Dominic urged. "I won't tell if you don't." He sensed Evrain's arrival at his shoulder. The kids all looked up with wide eyes and nervous giggles.

"Wow, how do you do that, Mr. Vampire?"

"I can't give away all my vampire secrets now, can I?" Evrain bared his fangs and the kids ran to their parents, screaming more from excitement than fear. As Dominic waved them off, he could hear the next group heading through the woods, chattering away.

"We going to have a busy evening. What did you do just now?"

"Just made a little fog." Evrain waggled his fingers.

"That's cheating!"

"But fun." Evrain gave him an evil grin. "This evening is going to be much more entertaining than I thought. If only our visitors knew the irony of the reality beneath the costume."

"It's a good thing they don't know they're visiting a real warlock," Dominic said. "We'd probably get run out of town." Shadow meowed her agreement. "Flaming torches, pitchforks, the works."

"Sounds fun."

They'd hardly shut the door before the next group arrived. For the next hour there was a steady stream of small witches, superheroes and one random kid dressed as a tomato.

As the last gaggle of children trailed down the path, Evrain turned off the fairy lights and blew out the candles. Inside, Dominic was doling out two more glasses of mulled cider.

"That's it," Evrain said, yawning. "If anyone else calls, we're out. The candy supply is decimated and all I want to do is sit down and snack." He put two more logs on the fire then slumped into one of the armchairs.

"Happy birthday!" Dominic walked over carrying a black cat-shaped cake on a plate, a single candle burning in its center. "Make a wish."

Evrain blew out the candle, grinning. "When on earth did you have time to make this?"

"I get to have some secrets too, you know. I hope it turned out okay." He nibbled his lower lip anxiously. "It was a recipe I hadn't tried before."

"Cut me a slice and we'll find out." The cake turned out to be a rich chocolate beneath the black icing, a layer of jam and buttercream running through its middle. The cat's green eyes were made from two pieces of crystallized lime and the whiskers from sugar strands. "Did Shadow model for you?"

"She was too busy trying to shove her face in the bowl of frosting. Blame her if you find a stray hair." Dominic cut two sizeable chunks of cake then handed one to Evrain on a pumpkin-patterned paper napkin. He watched while Evrain took a bite, waiting for his reaction.

"This is amazing." Evrain munched happily. "I think I may have to have another slice, though — for quality control purposes, you understand."

Dominic took a bite of his slice. "Not bad. I'm getting better at this baking thing."

They sat in companionable silence for a while, eating and drinking, absorbing the warmth from the fire. Finally, Evrain rubbed his stomach. "I'm full. That was all delicious. Thank you for putting it together, you've worked really hard today."

"I enjoyed doing it. Would you like your present now?"

"I thought all this was my present. You didn't have to get me anything else."

Dominic fetched a parcel, wrapped in brown paper and string, from the cupboard beneath the sink. He had decorated it with dried flower petals. He handed it over and Evrain pulled him down for a long, slow kiss.

"I hope you like it."

"It's from you, of course I'll like it." Evrain ripped off the paper. "It smells gorgeous." He squished the cushion between his hands releasing more of the scent. The applique cat on the cover was rotund, with a bushy tail, just like Shadow.

"It's got dried lavender and chamomile in it. I'm sorry, the sewing is not so great."

Evrain turned the cushion over in his hands examining every inch. "I recognize this fabric. It was in a box in the attic, wasn't it?"

"Yes, so were the jewels I used for the eyes."

"They catch the light." Flashes of light came from the green gems as Evrain turned the cushion toward the fire. "A cake and now a cushion, I love the cat theme."

"You've been having nightmares, and the herbs inside the pillow should help you sleep peacefully."

Evrain pulled Dominic into his arms. Dominic straddled his lap. "You're so perfect for me. I love you, Dominic Castine."

Dominic's mouth was dry and he didn't have the words to reply. He snuggled against Evrain's chest, tears springing to his eyes. He wished there was more he could do to help Evrain forget the warlock test, but it continued to haunt his dreams.

"I think it's time we went to bed, don't you? I'm going to strip you out of that costume very, very slowly."

Dominic swallowed, his cock jerking as much as it was able in the tight pants.

"It's my birthday, so I get to do what I want right?"

"I think I might regret saying this, but yes. Does this have anything to do with the wish you made when you blew out the candle?"

"Maybe." Evrain's eyes sparkled just as much as those on his gift. "Perhaps it's my turn to surprise you."

# Chapter Eleven

"I think we should indulge in role-play more often." Evrain admired the tableau he had created. Dominic, shirtless but still wearing the thigh boots and trousers from his pirate costume, lay spread-eagled on the bed. His wrists and ankles chained to the corner posts.

"If I'm the pirate, shouldn't you be my captive?" Dominic asked.

"Of course not. I was a rich paying passenger on your ship but you didn't know my true vampire nature. When you tried to rob me, I showed you the error of your ways. You, of course, had already forbidden members of your crew to come anywhere near your cabin, so you are completely at my mercy and by the end of the night you will be mine." Evrain gave a fake evil cackle worthy of any Vincent Price B-movie.

"And I suppose you stayed below decks during daylight hours to avoid being fried by the sun?"

"I'm such an ancient, powerful vampire that I can walk in the daylight, providing I cover my skin and wear sunglasses."

"Convenient, though I'm not sure pirates had sunglasses."

"Semantics."

Dominic tugged on his bonds. "And what exactly do you intend to do with me?"

"For a start, you will address me as 'my Lord.' I'm going to play with you a little to make sure you understand your position."

"But if I scream the place down, surely someone will hear?"

"Only the ship's cat, but she's bone idle. You do have a point, though." Evrain walked over to the dresser. The bottom drawer housed a collection of his favorite toys. He extracted a bit gag with wide leather straps. "This should do the job."

Dominic's eyes widened.

"Don't look at me like that—it was you who gave me the idea in the first place. Now lift your head so that I can buckle the strap." Evrain made sure the gag was tightly in place and smiled at the evil look Dominic was sending his way. "You have the most expressive eyes." He fished one of Shadow's discarded toys from beneath the bed—a small plastic ball with a bell inside that Shadow loved to chase. He pressed it into Dominic's hand. "You want me to stop, drop this. Blink if you understand." Dominic blinked, his copper lashes glinting in the low light of the bedside lamp.

"Time to get a little more comfortable." Evrain had already discarded the cloak and fangs but now he undid his shirt and slipped it off. The color rose on Dominic's cheeks. Evrain brushed the backs of his fingers across Dominic's face. "So warm, I'd bet good money that the rest of you is burning up too." He trailed his hand down Dominic's chest to the waistband of his trousers. He didn't undo them straightaway but slipped a finger beneath the waistband to touch the soft skin of Dominic's belly. Dominic's hips jerked, lifting his ass off the bed.

"Definitely in need of cooling down." A swift flick of the fingers dealt with the button then Evrain parted the zip. Dominic's rigid erection pushed at the fabric of his shorts. "It seems my prisoner isn't too bothered about his predicament." He levered the underwear down, hooking it under Dominic's balls. Dominic glared and mumbled around the gag.

"For a pirate, you have a very pretty cock, which deserves some decoration, but first I'm going to harness your balls." Evrain decided a running commentary would be good for his prisoner. He fetched the harness he intended to use. "You see one strap goes around your balls and one between them, then this buckle goes around the base of your cock. I think the tightest setting is appropriate, don't you?" Evrain closed the snaps with unrestrained glee. A light sheen of perspiration coated Dominic's skin and Evrain ran his finger through the moisture before flicking the tip of Evrain's cock. "It's always a little warm below decks." He gave Dominic's balls a light squeeze. "But now I have something really special for you." He held out his hand, displaying the shiny metal object that sat on his palm. The claw head urethral plug wouldn't be a surprise to Dominic because they had already discussed using it. Evrain had just been waiting for a good opportunity to get it out. He would never use anything on Dominic that he hadn't already agreed to.

"Pirates like their treasure, don't they? Silver and gold... It's going to look amazing and feel even better." The smooth, tapered plug was about two inches in length, much shorter than the sound, which they hadn't yet tried. Three ball-tipped arms would squeeze Dominic's cock head, pressing against his coronal ridge.

Evrain coated the plug with lube then, after checking Dominic's expression for any sign of distress, he inserted it. "I'll bet that feels good. Such a shame that cock ring means you won't get to come any time soon." He slowly twisted the claw so that the ball-tipped legs circled Dominic's cock head and the plug spun in his urethra. Behind the gag, Dominic moaned. He threw his head back and jerked his hips as if desperate for more friction.

"Perfect." Evrain stroked Dominic's balls, the separating strap between them pulling the skin taut. He explored further, reaching to apply pressure to the sensitive strip of skin behind Dominic's sac. "Of course, the disadvantage of chaining you down this way is that I can't get to your ass, but you'll be glad to know, I thought of that."

Dominic jerked and struggled, playing the part of the captive pirate to perfection.

"God, you look stunning. You turn my insides to mush when you let me do this."

Dominic blinked, his eyes bright with unshed tears. He clenched his fingers, tugging on the chains, sending a message about his impatience that Evrain get on with whatever he had planned.

"Patience, sweetheart. The more you struggle, the more I like it." With a whisper of power, Evrain unsealed the locks holding the manacles around Dominic's ankles closed. He pulled two long, buckled straps from beneath the mattress then hooked them around the posts at the head of the bed. He passed one strap under Dominic's thigh, just beneath his knee, then cinched the leather through the buckle. It was an effective way of pulling Dominic's knee back almost to his chest, lifting his ass off the bed a fraction. When Evrain completed the exercise on the other side, Dominic was supported but held open and accessible. Except for his pants. *Damn.*

Not wanting to appear as though he hadn't planned appropriately, Evrain fetched a pair of nail scissors from the bathroom. "I promise not to nick anything important, providing you keep still." He took his time slitting the seams of Dominic's pirate costume and underwear until the tattered rags could be pulled from under Dominic's body, leaving him bare apart from the thigh boots.

"I could come just from looking at you." Evrain shoved a hand down the front of his leather pants to give his cock a squeeze. The pain shifted him back from the brink. *Should have put a cock ring on me too.* He manipulated the air to form a circle around the base of his shaft, applying just enough pressure to buy himself some time. *Gregory wouldn't approve of me using my power like this, but it's all good practice.* Thickening air required a delicate touch.

Watching him, Dominic grinned around the gag.

"Laugh it up, Captain Sparrow. You just bought yourself a night in chastity." Evrain wiped away a little drool that had gathered at the corner of Dominic's mouth. "Someone needs to invent a gag that's less messy." He checked the claw covering the head of Dominic's cock. The three claw arms were a perfect fit, each of the little balls applying enough pressure to be stimulating. He gave it a twist, eliciting a strangled moan from Dominic.

"We definitely need to experiment with sounds. If this short insert makes you so sensitive, imagine what a full-length steel rod would do."

Dominic thrashed his head from side to side.

"We'll see."

Evrain debated whether or not to strip off his leathers, but Dominic loved the way they clung to his thighs so he decided to leave them on. He grabbed a pot of homemade lube and a stone dildo from the dresser. "Time to slick you up, love." He swirled the polished granite rod in the lube, making sure it was well coated before pressing the tip to Dominic's hole. He teased him with the tip, making the surrounding skin glossy, before pushing the first inch or so inside. Dominic's cock slapped his belly, pre-cum gleaming around the claw. The skin of his balls, trapped in the harness, was smooth and taut. Heat came off his skin, furnace hot.

"You're so ready for me, aren't you?" Evrain pushed the dildo home, pumping it a few times to make sure Dominic's channel was well-coated with lube. Dominic squeezed his eyes shut and a single tear escaped from beneath an eyelid. Fucking Dominic's slick hole with the dildo was fun but Evrain couldn't wait to get inside him. Unzipping his pants was a huge relief. He withdrew the toy from Dominic's grasping channel then smeared his cock with more lube. The jar and toy were swept to the floor when he clambered onto the bed, positioning himself between Dominic's widespread thighs.

"A real vampire would bite you, make you too weak to resist." Evrain leaned forward and pressed his teeth into the flesh around one of Dominic's hardened nipples. He bit just hard enough to leave a mark. "You should always have my marks on you. I'm going to make that a rule." He licked his way down Dominic's abs, which flexed and twitched beneath his tongue. Dominic's familiar scent, his taste, his silken skin… Evrain couldn't wait any longer. He lined up his cock and pushed inside Dominic's body in one smooth thrust. Fully seated, he held still, taking a few deep breaths. He had made love to Dominic hundreds of times but this moment, when they were joined, never failed to take his breath away.

"So good. So mine. Gonna hold you prisoner forever." He jacked his hips, too close to the edge to be gentle. His control faltered and the ring of air around his cock dissipated. The release of pressure made him dizzy and only a huge effort of will kept him from collapsing across Dominic's body. He had the presence of mind to unsnap the harness around Dominic's balls and remove the claw.

"Together."

Any hope of grace was lost. Evrain shuddered as he came, taking Dominic with him. Dominic's back arched, his body pulled Evrain deeper, destroying any semblance of control Evrain might have clung on to. "Fuck, fuck, fuck." It was hard to focus, to think. Pulling free came with regret but he needed to release Dominic's legs, undo the gag and massage his jaw. The wrist chains came last then, duty done, Evrain collapsed into Dominic's embrace.

"Why are you holding me?" he muttered. "Should be the other way around."

"Who made that rule, because it's a stupid one? Can I take the boots off now, because they aren't the most comfortable thing to have on in bed?"

"Sure. But we're keeping them."

"Well, as you destroyed my pants, the costume shop is going to be charging us anyway. You can explain what happened when you take that cloak back."

"You don't want me to keep the cloak? I could amp up the whole warlock thing with a costume — doesn't have to be a vampire."

"No. You're quite warlocky enough without a costume. I really need to take another shower."

"Good idea. With all that water we can pretend I'm making you walk your own plank unless you grant me sexual favors."

"How long are you going to keep this up?"

"Really? That's the line you came up with? This is way too easy." Evrain laughed as he rolled off the bed.

"It's your birthday. I'm being kind."

"Perhaps we should forget the shower for a while and make use of the leftover cake."

"I'm… No. Just no. The bed would be full of crumbs."

"Spoilsport." Evrain pouted.

"There is some leftover frosting…"

"Stay here. I'll be five seconds." Frosting and a naked Dominic were a combination too good to resist.

# Chapter Twelve

"What are you looking at on there?" Evrain leaned over Dominic's shoulder to nosy at his laptop screen. Dominic, his legs curled under him, had been sat in the armchair next to the fire for the last hour.

"Well, you remember when Gregory was telling you about the purpose of warlocks? I decided to do a bit of research. I'm beginning to wish I hadn't. I know this isn't particularly scientific, but there's a list here of ten potential natural disasters that could happen at any time. Four of them are in North America."

Evrain took the seat on the other side of the fire. "I should lecture you about looking into things that might never happen, but I'm intrigued. What have you got?"

"Well, there are a couple in Japan, another big earthquake with a tsunami and the possibility that Mount Fuji might erupt. There's a volcano in Iceland, which is another place where the entire country seems to be bubbling with lava. A big earthquake off the coast of Chile, a huge tsunami in the Caribbean, solar storms…"

"It sounds like we are all doomed," Evrain said. "What about closer to home?"

"Wildfires is the first thing. It seems that the season is going to get longer and fiercer. It says here that the Forestry Service has recorded that since 1999, the acreage burned by wildfires in the US has tripled annually. That's scary, but inevitable with climate change, I suppose."

"There have been a few more of those back home in the UK with the recent dry summers," Evrain said, staring into the dancing flames in the hearth. "I can't imagine what it's like to get caught in one." Sparks spat from the fireplace.

"Stop thinking about it or you'll set this place alight."

"Sorry." Evrain gave him a sheepish smile.

"Some people seem to think that the east coast will eventually be underwater because the sea level is increasing, rising three or four times faster than anywhere else in the world."

"Then it's a good job we don't live in New York."

"Evrain! You of all people should take this more seriously. The next one is more obvious, the big one could arrive any time."

"Forgive me, what do you mean by the big one?"

"An earthquake in California, somewhere on the San Andreas fault."

"It's happened before, hasn't it? So I suppose the chances of it happening again are quite high."

"Yes, the damage would be catastrophic, but that's not the one on this list that worries me the most. It says here that it is likely an eight to nine magnitude earthquake and tsunami will occur off the coast of Oregon within the next fifty years. If it happens it could kill over ten thousand people and split apart portions of the west coast."

"Your hands are shaking." Evrain launched from his chair to kneel in front of Dominic.

"Do you think it's a coincidence that Gregory arranged for you to live here?"

"I don't know, he's never said anything specific. If something like that happened there'd be very little I could do about it."

"That's not the point though, is it? Gregory said it's not averting huge natural disasters that warlocks are here for, it's about making their impact less disastrous."

"I don't think it's something you should be worrying about. There's always a chance this kind of thing will happen — it's happening all over the world every day, after all. There's always some storm or eruption or flood... Warlocks aren't like superheroes from films, rushing around saving lives. Though I'd look good in one of those costumes." Diffusing the tension was the right thing to do because Dominic chuckled. He closed the lid of his laptop.

"Who would you want to be? I'm not sure about the whole tights thing. But they all seem to go for skin-tight outfits." He put his laptop on the floor.

"Shift over." Evrain pulled Dominic from the chair, took his place then settled him into his lap. "I don't know, I think my personality is closest to Deadpool but I'm not sure about the red outfit."

"You're certainly sarcastic enough. But I can see you all in black, so who would that be?"

"Batman, or one of the X-Men?"

"Yum! Lots of black leather and armor would definitely suit you."

"I didn't know you had a leather fetish." Evrain stroked a strand of hair away from Dominic's cheek.

"Everyone likes the smell of leather, don't they? I love the smell of rubber as well. Put me in a tire shop and I'm happy."

"In that case, perhaps we should get a hot water bottle for the bed."

"I have you. I don't need any other source of heat at night, that's for sure." Dominic nuzzled Evrain's neck. "Have you seen Shadow? She usually appears when there's a fire going but I haven't seen her all day."

"I think she has a boyfriend," Evrain replied. "She went out last night and when I went to call her in there was no sign of her. She wandered in this morning, scoffed her food then went upstairs to the spare room and she's been there ever since. Sleeping off whatever it was she got up to."

"Good for her, she should be out having fun. If she has some of Aggie's spirit in her, Lord knows what she's getting up to." Dominic grinned.

"Changing the subject completely, are you looking forward to everyone getting together for Thanksgiving?" Evrain asked.

"Sure, we haven't seen Damon and Nathaniel for a while. Where are we going to put them all?"

"I should have told you," Evrain said. "When Gregory called last night he said that he and Coryn are going to stay in that posh hotel they like in Portland, so Damon and Nate can stay here."

"That's cool. I suppose in a pinch we could put an inflatable mattress down here to free up our room, but I'd rather we got to sleep in our own bed. I'm looking forward to doing all the cooking, it's going to be fun."

"I suppose we'll have to do a huge grocery run." Evrain shuddered. "I hate supermarkets."

"I've done an online order, which will get delivered two days before. I want to do some of the preparation in advance so that I'm not stuck in the kitchen all day on the day itself."

"I'm impressed," Evrain said. "That kind of organization deserves a reward."

"What kind of reward?"

"Why do you sound so suspicious?"

"Because I know you. Your idea of a reward usually involves me on my knees, calling you Sir." He rolled his eyes comically.

"I'm missing your point here." Evrain flicked open the stud on Dominic's waistband then slipped his hand down the front of his pants. "You're hard."

Dominic laughed. "So are you, and you've been pushing that steel rod of yours into my ass since you sat me on your lap, so what do you expect?"

"Submission. Obedience."

"Then your expectations exceed reality. I'm busy." Despite his words, Dominic thrust into Evrain's hand. "I have recipes to check, silverware to clean, the bathroom needs a scrub and I haven't made up the guest room bed yet."

"Damon can do that when he gets here."

"I'm not having our guests making their own beds! And I want to dig some mulch into the new raised bed at the back of the house."

Evrain massaged Dominic's cock. "If you can talk about mulch when I'm doing this, I must be doing it wrong."

"Sorry. I have a lot on my mind." Dominic sucked in his breath.

"And it's my job to clear that busy head of yours. I want your focus on me for a while. Selfish, I know, but I don't care." Evrain dug his nail into Dominic's slit. "I'm going to bind this nice and tight, tie your hands behind your back so you can't touch."

"And?" Dominic's voice was higher pitched than usual.

"I think we should make more use of the spreader bar under the bed, don't you? I'm going to spread you wide then play with your pretty hole for a while. Then…well, you'll have to wait and see. I'm not giving away all my kinky secrets in one go." He gave Dominic's dick a final tug. "I'm going to get some water. You go upstairs, strip, then wait for me on the bed. Head down, ass up."

"Such a sweet talker." Dominic clambered off Evrain's lap, his fly open, rigid dick jutting out. "Don't be long or I might be tempted to get a head start."

"Touch my property and you'll feel the kiss of my cane instead of my lips — and that's not an idle threat." He rose with deceptive languor.

"I know…Sir."

Dominic took the stairs two at a time. Evrain went to the kitchen and filled a glass jug with water from the tap. He knocked a whole tray of ice cubes into it, grabbed a couple of tumblers then followed Dominic upstairs.

The most perfect sight met him when he went into the bedroom. Dominic's obedience was a thrill in itself, but his submissive pose was the cherry on a delicious, three-layer, fresh cream and strawberries cake. Evrain licked his lips. *Fuck, I'm the luckiest warlock in the world.* He was tempted to throw all his plans out of the window and fuck Dominic right away. However, drawing out their mutual pleasure might try his patience, but it was worth it to glimpse the expression on Dominic's face when he was finally permitted to come.

The spreader bar had been pulled from beneath the bed but left on the floor. Evrain tapped the inside of Dominic's bare leg, encouraging him to spread a little wider. He positioned the bar between his legs before fastening each of the leather cuffs on the ends around Dominic's ankles. Dominic gave the sweetest whimper, fisting the bed clothes, already worked up. The prospect of bondage always did that to him — something that Evrain loved. He found a pair of soft, Velcro-fastening cuffs, using them to bind Dominic's hands behind his back. It put him in an awkward position, fighting for balance. Evrain made sure there wasn't too much strain on Dominic's neck and that the pillow under his face wasn't suffocating him.

"Comfortable?"

"No!"

"Excited?" Evrain didn't get a response. "I can see you are." He reached beneath Dominic's body to grasp his cock. "This is a giveaway."

Dominic squirmed as best he was able, attempting to get away from Evrain's grip.

"Now, now. Keep still or you'll fall off the bed and I don't want you damaging anything important."

"You're so considerate."

"I know." Evrain stripped to his underwear, enjoying the cool air on his heated skin. He was just as worked up as Dominic. He grabbed lube from the dresser, coated two fingers then pressed them to Dominic's hole. A few whispered words heated the slick and his fingers slid into Dominic's body.

"So warm." Dominic's inner muscles gripped him. "What did you do to the lube?"

"Just a little heat."

"I like it."

Evrain moved his fingers, probing, stretching.

"Oh God." Dominic's breath hitched. "More. So good."

Evrain added a third finger, shifting them back and forth fast enough to sensitize Dominic's passage but not fast enough to make him come untouched. "Love being inside you, fingers or cock, touching where no one else gets to touch." He gave Dominic's ass a sharp smack before pulling clear. Dominic's breath came in sharp, rapid gasps, his fingers furled and unfurled, grasping at the air.

"Come back! What are you doing?"

"It's a surprise." Evrain slipped his hand into the jug of iced water. He grabbed one slippery cube then, without warning, pressed it to Dominic's entrance.

"Holy fuck!" Dominic twisted, in a vain attempt to see what Evrain was doing. "You bastard."

"That's 'you bastard, Sir.'" He pushed the melting cube inside Dominic's body. Water dripped, rolling in shimmering lines down Dominic's thighs. Evrain stroked them away, warming his fingers on Dominic's skin. "First heat, then ice. Fire and water, two of my favorite elements." He released Dominic's wrists, concerned that the strain on his shoulders might be too much as his muscles flexed in response to the shock. He pushed up on his arms, making a bridge. The side of his face that Evrain could see was flushed pink. "Looks like you need cooling down a bit more." He fished for another cube of ice then reached beneath Dominic's body to rub it over his nipples.

Dominic keened and attempted to hump the bed but with his legs forcibly spread it wasn't possible. Evrain chuckled but fun as it was to see Dominic struggle, getting inside him was the main goal. The last time Evrain had tried to fuck Dominic while he was attached to the spreader bar, Evrain had ended up with bruised knees. He wasn't going to make that mistake again, so he worked the buckles free.

"Nobody explains that bondage can be a real cock blocker. You get all worked up playing with ropes and chains but then find you've restricted your own access."

"Stop talking about yourself in the second person and fuck me," Dominic grunted. "You've had your fun. I think I deserve mine. Sir."

"Such insubordination. For that I should make you wait."

"You wouldn't!"

Evrain pressed the tip of his lube-slicked cock to Dominic's hole. "Just want you to know it's a possibility." He pushed inside Dominic's channel then stilled. "Jesus, that's cold!"

Dominic fell about laughing and Evrain slipped free of his body. "Laugh it up, green fingers. What did you expect?"

Dominic had a fit of the giggles and couldn't stop.

"Keep still or I'll amuse myself jacking off." Evrain gave his cock a few rubs, warming it. He repositioned himself and tried again. This time, the cold wasn't unexpected. It still took a while to get used to the difference from Dominic's usual welcoming warmth. *I need to rethink my timing if I use ice again, maybe follow up with some ginger.* Beneath him, Dominic whimpered. Evrain flipped him over, wanting to look into his eyes as Dominic came. He moved slowly, taking his time, wringing every ounce of pleasure out of each movement. He bent Dominic's leg back, changing his angle to get deeper.

"Love this. Love you." Evrain clasped one of Dominic's hands, lacing their fingers together. As his orgasm built, he moved faster, watching Dominic's expression. Dominic's lips parted and Evrain couldn't resist leaning in for a kiss. Pleasure built and he groaned. "Together?"

Dominic blinked. "Soon. Can't wait…"

They were so well matched, Dominic's body so familiar, Evrain knew exactly when Dominic reached the point of no return. Shuddering, he came, reaching for his cock to draw out the orgasm. Evrain knocked his hand away.

"That's mine." The sensation of Dominic's pulsing shaft locked in a cage of his fingers was enough to bring Evrain to climax. With a final, powerful thrust, he came. A strange sensation of falling overwhelmed him. He went with it, accepted it, barely aware of his body other than where he and Dominic were joined, intimately and hand in hand. His vision blurred. Sated, he collapsed onto Dominic, smearing his skin with Dominic's release.

"I…" He couldn't find words. Engaging his brain to come up with connected sentences was too much of a challenge. He settled for moving to the side so that he wouldn't crush Dominic, pulling him close so they were touching as much as possible. For now, words were unnecessary. All the communication they needed was in their touch.

# Chapter Thirteen

"What in the world possessed us to host Thanksgiving here?" Dominic ran flour-dusted fingers through his already tangled hair. "They'll be arriving soon and I'm nowhere near ready."

Evrain, deciding that self-preservation was an imperative, didn't remind Dominic that it had been his idea. "And when they do, you'll have an army of helpers. None of them are the kind of people to sit around watching you do all the work." He pressed against Dominic's back, encircling him with his arms. "Relax. This is supposed to be a fun, laid-back day with friends. There's no need to get stressed." He gave Dominic's ass a squeeze.

"I want everything to be perfect." Dominic pushed back against him.

"And it will be." Evrain planted a few nibbling kisses on Dominic's neck. "The smells alone tell me that. Now, what can I do to help?"

"Stop molesting me for a start."

"But that's the fun part." Evrain slipped a hand up Dominic's shirt until he found a nipple to pinch. "I should have put clamps on these while you cooked."

"Uh, no, you shouldn't. I wouldn't have been able to focus enough to read Aggie's recipes, let alone pull them all together."

"True. My stomach would never forgive me."

"You can mash the potatoes while I mix the honey sesame dressing for the carrots. I have an insulated dish waiting for the mash. The butter's out and I already chopped the parsley to stir into it."

Evrain let him go with some reluctance. "Nate and Damon are bringing dessert, right?"

"Yes. I left it up to them what they brought. Gregory and Coryn are bringing wine. You can carve the turkey at the table. All the vegetables are ready, cranberry sauce is in the fridge. What have I forgotten?" He spun around the kitchen, pulling open doors and checking dishes. "Bread sauce!"

"That's a last-minute thing, though… It can wait," Evrain said. "These spuds are done."

"Thanks. Can you check the table?"

The dark red tablecloth Dominic had found at the back of the linen closet set off the white crockery and antique silverware perfectly. He'd pulled together a spray of evergreen foliage from the garden, adding color with some holly berries and late salvia. Mats were set out ready for the hot dishes along with strategically placed serving spoons.

"Just salt and pepper missing, I think." Evrain fetched the cruet set from a cupboard. The cottage was warm enough but he tweaked the fire anyway, creating a shower of sparks and earning a glare from Shadow, who had been snoozing on the rug.

"Fat, lazy mammal. I can't believe you ate all those giblets in one go." He bent to give her a stroke and she rolled onto her back, exposing her ample belly. Evrain obliged by getting down on his knees to pet her. "You're so spoiled." Rumbling purrs sent vibrations through his hand until she rolled away.

As he got to his feet there was a knock at the door. He gave Dominic a reassuring grin and went to open it. All four of their guests piled in at once, bringing a blast of frigid air with them. Bags, bottles and boxes were dumped on every surface so that hugs could be delivered and received.

Evrain took everyone's coats upstairs then returned to find the corkscrew.

"Lunch is almost ready, but we have time for a pre-meal drink. Is red wine okay with everyone? This looks like a really nice bottle, Gregory." Evrain hefted one of several bottles Gregory had put on the kitchen counter.

"From a friend who runs a vineyard in California. He holds back the best stuff for himself and a few select friends. I dealt with an irrigation problem he was having a few years back and he's never forgotten — sends a couple of cases every now and then."

"That's because you waggled your fingers and tripled his profits." Coryn reached for a glass. "Hardly a great effort."

"Yes, my love. You and I know that, but he thinks I spent weeks surveying his land, taking boreholes tests and using complex computer models to come up with a solution to his problem. I didn't charge him nearly as much as I could have and he feels guilty about it. I'm happy to drink his penance." They clinked glasses.

"Damon, you want a glass?" Evrain asked.

Damon scuffed his toe into the rug, casting a glance at Nathaniel.

"Ah. Nate, is it okay for Damon to have small glass of wine?" Evrain redirected his question.

"Just the one. I'm in a benevolent mood and he behaved himself on the journey. Even listened to my favorite country music in the car without making any sarcastic comments."

Damon beamed and accepted the glass Evrain offered him. His free hand strayed to the thick leather collar around his neck. "Thank you, Master."

"You deserve an entire bottle to yourself for holding your tongue under such trying circumstances," Coryn said. "Nate has the worst taste in music ever."

Damon tried, and failed, to hide his grin.

"Why don't you go and see what you can do to help Dominic? And don't listen to Coryn—he's talking trash." Nathaniel grabbed Damon's thick black hair and gave him a fierce kiss before releasing him. Damon scurried over to Dominic, his face bright red.

Evrain gave Nate a knowing glance. "It's a shame Felix couldn't join us." Nathaniel's long-suffering driver was part of their extended family too.

"He has a new girlfriend and apparently, every now and again, I'm supposed to give him time off. Most inconvenient."

Evrain chuckled. "Things have progressed with you and Damon too, I see."

"I'm channeling through him now. He still needs discipline, but considering his past, he's willing to learn. I'm pleased with him." Nate didn't lower his voice and Evrain could see the blush on Damon's cheeks from across the room. "Doesn't mean he won't get his nightly spanking of course."

"Of course." Evrain gave thanks that the cottage had thick walls.

Coryn, Nate and Gregory settled with their drinks in chairs around the fire. Evrain had heaved two extras from the bedrooms down the stairs at the cost of quite a few bruises and a lot of cursing. There wasn't room for more but plenty of cushions would allow a couple of people to sit on the floor in relative comfort. He took a glass of wine over to Dominic.

"You can take a break for a few minutes."

"I don't…"

"I can keep an eye on everything," Damon offered. "Go relax for a while."

"It's just the gravy and bread sauce. I *could* use a break."

"Uh, Dominic, what's bread sauce?" Damon prodded at the contents of the pan.

"One of Evrain's Brit imports. Apparently you can't eat turkey without it."

"You can't," Evrain confirmed. "Wait until you try it, it's good."

Dominic took the offered glass then swallowed a large mouthful. "Oh, that's wonderful." Evrain led him over to the fire, took a seat then pulled him onto his lap.

"Careful." Dominic swung an arm, trying to keep his wineglass balanced. On the rug, Shadow stretched out her front paws, then her back ones. She settled onto her side, stomach to the fire.

"She knows where she's well off," Nate commented.

"Evrain thinks he's in charge," Dominic said, "but in this house, Shadow rules with an iron paw."

"She does not," Evrain protested.

"And who drove an extra five miles to a different market to find the particular brand of canned tuna she likes the best?"

"In my defense, I gave her some of that other stuff and she looked at me like she was about to commit murder." He nipped at Dominic's earlobe. "And for that, you'll be punished later." He traced the line of Dominic's throat with the back of his hand. "You'd look good with a collar wrapped around here."

Dominic glanced across at Damon, who was stirring the bread sauce and bopping along to the radio providing background music. "In your dreams."

"The best kind of dreams."

Coryn and Gregory exchanged a knowing glance and Nate chuckled.

"What?" Evrain glared at his guests.

"Good to see that you are firmly under thumb and paw, Evrain," Nate said. "Young warlocks have a tendency to arrogance, you're lucky to have companions to keep you in your place."

Dominic laughed and took another sip of wine. "Shadow's better at it than I am."

"Um, I think this bread sauce is about done, Dominic," Damon called from the kitchen.

"On my way." Dominic slid from Evrain's lap. "If you all want to get situated around the table, the food is on its way. Damon, do you mind helping me bring everything to the table?"

"Sure. It all looks so scrummy."

Between Damon and Dominic, they transported multiple dishes of food to the table and gave out plates that had been warming in the bottom of the oven. Evrain sat at the head of the table with Gregory opposite. Everyone else took their seats next to their partners.

"Before we all descend on this wonderful food," Gregory said, "I'd like to make a short toast." He raised his glass and the others followed suit. "Let's give thanks for love." His eyes twinkled as he looked at Coryn. "To friendship and to making the world a better place."

"Hear, hear." The clink of crystal rang in the air as they all joined in the toast.

"Then let's eat!" Evrain stood, picked up a pair of carving knives and set to on the turkey while everyone else helped themselves from the various dishes. For the next hour they ate, drank, chatted and laughed like normal people.

When they were done and Evrain didn't think he could fit another crumb into his stomach, Dominic put the cheese and wine on a low table next to the fire. Nate and Damon insisted on clearing the table and washing up, saying that Dominic had done enough already. Evrain made coffee then grabbed a tea towel to help dry. When all that was left was the roasting tin soaking in the sink, they gathered around the fire, Damon on cushions at Nate's feet, Dominic in Evrain's lap.

"Could you tell us all about your test?" Damon asked, receiving a clip around the ear from Nate for his impertinence.

"It's not your place to ask Evrain to talk about such a personal matter," Nate said. Damon bit his lip and bowed his head.

"Sorry, Evrain."

"It's fine," Evrain said. "I don't mind, and who knows? It might not be too long before the two of you have to face your own test. I'm not sure our story will help you because, according to Gregory, every test is very different. I wouldn't wish what happened to us on anyone." Telling the story one more time was cathartic. Evrain had gone over and over the events in his head, trying to work out how where he could have done anything different. Recounting events out loud, hearing others' opinions, helped him accept that the test had been out of his control.

"And I suppose that's what I hate most about what happened," he said, finishing his story. "Feeling utterly helpless."

"You weren't completely helpless, though, were you? Sounds like you did an amazing job," Nate said.

"And the test was far, far tougher than the one Coryn and I faced," Gregory added. "Killian really went to town."

"Do you think there was a reason for that?" Dominic asked. "I mean, I thought that though the tests are different, aren't they set up to be equally challenging for every warlock?"

"I thought so, until now." Gregory reached for Coryn's hand, giving it a squeeze. "But you are exceptionally powerful, Evrain. I imagine it was felt that a harsher challenge was needed in your case." He shrugged. "Who knows? The whole process is shrouded in mystery and I can't see that changing any time soon."

"Have you come any closer to deciding what your strongest element is, Evrain?" Nate asked. "Mine is air. Gregory's is water. What about you?"

Evrain stroked Dominic's thigh. "I'm still not sure. I thought fire, or earth, but to be honest, I don't feel that much different using any of them. Fire has the most appeal, but I think that's probably the visual stimulus."

He flicked his fingers toward the fire and the flames rose higher. "Instant satisfaction."

Gregory shook his head. "An artistic, creative temperament can be a problem. I'm much more pragmatic than you are. But I think that has come with age."

"You still have your moments," Coryn said, smiling.

"You have a delicate touch with air, love," Dominic said, "from what I've witnessed, but you also have an affinity for the earth."

"It's the easiest to feel. It's like each element has its own personality. Fire is wild, it doesn't want to be controlled. Air dances, it likes to show off, to move around. Earth is slower, friendly, warm…it seems to have a sense of its own strength and tries to subdue it. Water is challenging, it wants to grow, take over. Spread itself. But it's not so difficult to manipulate, at least in reasonable quantities." He met Gregory's eyes, then Nathaniel's. "Am I talking utter codswallop?"

"To me, and I think to Nate, the elements are tools that we are fortunate to be able to use. You have a much closer affinity with each of them and that's what gives you your power. You persuade the elements to cooperate with you. Whereas we bludgeon them into submission."

Nate nodded. "Succinct, but true. I have to get quite violent to convince the winds to go where I want them to. There's no way I could manage the same thing with fire."

"Am I the only one thinking this conversation is surreal?" Damon piped up. He leaned forward to pet Shadow, who was still curled up on the rug. She nosed at his hand then hauled herself up, moving to sit on his lap.

"When you live with a warlock, you get used to it," Coryn said. "We should set up a self-help group for warlock partners, maybe Skype each other once a week to compare notes."

"I think that's a great idea," Dominic said.

"Me too! Can we get a cat, Master? Every warlock should have a cat, right?" Damon scratched one of Shadow's velvet ears. She purred, nuzzling, asking for more.

"Shameless hussy," Dominic said. "You've discovered her soft spot. She loves having her ears scratched more than anything, but watch out for her belly. She'll lie on her back with her legs in the air, that soft tummy all tempting. Then the instant you stroke it she turns into a Venus fly cat with four sets of claws and her teeth clamped around your arm."

"I don't believe it," Damon said. "She's such a sweet kitty." Shadow licked his hand.

"To answer your question, brat, I wouldn't mind having a fur ball around the house. When we get home we'll go to the local shelter and you can pick one out."

"Really?" Damon vibrated with excitement. "This is the best Thanksgiving ever."

"I'll email about a weekly get-together," Coryn said. "Then Damon can show us his new pet."

Evrain exchanged looks first with Gregory, then Nathaniel. "We are so fucked." He mouthed the words silently but got wry nods of agreement from them both.

"On another subject," Nate said, "and I hope you don't mind me asking, Dominic, but how much pain do you feel when Evrain channels through you? Damon is finding it quite uncomfortable."

"I won't pretend it's not painful," Dominic admitted. "It's debilitating enough that I have to stop work after a while. I had flu once and it's similar—the muscle aches, I mean. I think it has been getting a bit easier, though."

"Whereas I hardly feel anything at all," Coryn said.

"That comes with age and wisdom," Gregory said. "Though I think Dominic has a hard time of it because Evrain is so powerful. He's still learning to control what he can do. When he's mastered his abilities, I'm sure it will get easier. As for Damon, I think it's the case that Nathaniel has been too used to having to manage his power without a partner to channel through. The pair of you just need more practice being together then things will ease. A warlock's partner has to be very strong. It's not easy dealing with such an unusual lifestyle. But, if it helps, once a warlock has met his life partner, his loyalty is guaranteed."

"To me it feels like I'm being shocked... Lots of tiny electric shocks all over my body and I go jerky." Damon nibbled on his lower lip. "I must be a freak. It never happened when I was with…"

"Symeon. You can say his name, Damon." Nathaniel tousled Damon's hair. "We are working through a few issues regarding Damon's past, but he's getting there."

"Things are getting far too serious around here," Coryn said. "Someone hand me a plate because I intend to gorge myself on cheese." He licked his lips and the bleak mood was broken.

# Chapter Fourteen

Evrain and Dominic woke late the following morning, slightly the worse for wear.

"Things got pretty intense yesterday," Dominic said, running his fingers down Evrain's chest. "Coryn knows exactly how to defuse a situation, though, doesn't he?"

"I imagine he's had a lot of practice with Gregory." Evrain shifted, throwing one arm across the pillow. "That man cannot be easy to live with."

"When we get to their age, I hope we're still as much in love as they are."

"That's not in doubt." Evrain yawned. "That was some late night. I feel like I've only had a couple of hours sleep. My head hurts too."

Dominic checked the clock. "It's called a hangover and it's almost ten — you've had seven hours. Nathaniel is quite the card shark, isn't he?"

"It's a good job we were playing for Cheetos, otherwise you and I would be destitute by now. I swear that man can see right through the cards."

"Could he? Is that possible?"

"I think the plastic coating on the cards might be a problem. If they had been older-style ones, just paper and ink, it might be possible, but that kind of focus would have required him to channel and Damon wasn't showing any sign of that. I think we both have to face up to the fact that we are rubbish at poker."

"Maybe Shadow was helping in some way. She sat on Damon's lap all evening and he was next to Nate."

"Now that I could believe. That animal will do anything for food and Nate was sneaking her bits of cheese most of the night."

"We had fun, though, didn't we? Good company, good food... We have a lot to be thankful for."

"We do. And I had a great time. You did an amazing job with the food."

"Talking of, I should get up and sort out some breakfast before Nate and Damon make an appearance."

"Damon is quite capable of finding his way around a fridge. Pretty sure he can boil an egg if he needs to. I'd much prefer you to stay here in bed with me than slaving in the kitchen, though a mug of coffee would go down well. Which, I will make. You did all the hard work yesterday." He threw back the covers, revealing a straining erection.

"Oh, yum!" Before Evrain could move and take away his treat, Dominic slithered down the bed. "Coffee can wait." He plunged his mouth over Evrain's straining shaft, taking him as deep as he could. He loved the power that giving Evrain a blow job gave him, adored the sounds that Evrain made as he fought to hold back his orgasm. Evrain made no attempt to take control. Often he would wind his fingers through Dominic's hair and hold him in place. This morning, he let Dominic have his way.

Dominic sucked, kissed and nibbled until Evrain was squirming and crying for release. He mouthed his balls in turn, sucking and kissing the tender, heated flesh.

"You taste so good."

"Dom… I need…"

"I know you do." Dominic paused to grin at his lover before resuming his task. The taste of Evrain's pre-cum flooded Dominic's mouth. Evrain grunted, his muscles tensing. After a few more soothing licks to his balls, Dominic nibbled his way from one end of Evrain's shaft to the other before focusing his attention on the head, where he knew Evrain was most sensitive. He ran his tongue around the tip then sucked the head again and again.

"Dominic!"

His name being screamed was all the warning Dominic got before Evrain came in a hot gush into his throat. He swallowed and licked a bit more, drawing the last threads of orgasm from Evrain's body. When his shudders stopped, Dominic gave Evrain's dick a final kiss before crawling up his body to plant another kiss on his lips.

"You taste of me." Evrain reached between them to grasp Dominic's cock. "Your turn."

"Hard and fast," Dominic urged. He loved the feeling of Evrain's spell-calloused fingers wrapped around his cock. Evrain obliged with a few aggressive jerks, bringing him over the edge in a rush of pleasure. Dominic sagged against him, drawing a few ragged breaths.

"Now I want that coffee," Dominic said.

"Just give me a moment to recover, brat." Evrain delivered a couple of sharp slaps to Dominic's bare ass.

"Stop that. What's that noise? Can you hear something?" Dominic strained to listen to the sounds coming from somewhere across the landing. "Oh…"

"It sounds like Nate is delivering quite the spanking over there," Evrain muttered. "He must have a permanently sore palm dealing with Damon."

"Damon has changed a lot under Nate's care, though, hasn't he?"

"They fit each other well. I have to admit that surprises me. I didn't realize Nate had quite such a kinky streak, but he's dominant enough to keep Damon under control. Fate's a funny thing, isn't it? Who'd have thought they'd have ended up together?"

"I admire Damon's strength. He suffered at Symeon's hands and he was far too young to have gone through that kind of abuse. It's remarkable that he's pulled back the way he has. I think they need each other."

"As we do."

"The warlock world works in mysterious ways. Everything seems fated, don't you think?"

"Maybe. After what we've seen and been through since I came into my power, I don't think anything will ever surprise me again. I think I may need to start wearing the bracelet again."

"That's good, isn't it? It means you're back to full strength." Dominic petted Evrain's hair.

"I suppose. I wish there was another way to dampen the power. I'll ask Nate this morning. Maybe he can come up with something. But in the meantime" — Evrain swung his legs out of bed —"there's a coffee craving that needs to be satisfied and no doubt a starving cat to feed. I'll come back for a shower after breakfast."

Dominic enjoyed the view as Evrain wriggled into a pair of jeans and a T-shirt.

"Stop watching my ass."

"Nope, that's one order I'll never obey." Dominic grinned. "I'll take a quick shower then come join you." He didn't get out of bed, but snuggled back beneath the covers with a happy sigh. He had a feeling it was going to be a good day.

* * * *

"If it's okay with you guys that we impose on your hospitality for another night, Damon and I would like to hang around. It's been an age since I had a break and the hiking around here is spectacular." Nate sipped his second cup of coffee, his free hand resting on Damon's thigh.

"Of course, stay as long as you like," Evrain offered. "I have today and tomorrow off work. Dominic probably has a few things to take care of in the garden, but we could come with you in a bit. It's a nice day for a hike."

"Do you have any suggestions about where we could go?" Nathaniel asked. "I don't know the area well — I've only ever visited the cottage or Portland. We get out in the wilds when we can, from San Francisco, but it's not as often as I'd like."

"I love taking walks among the redwoods," Damon said. "They are beautiful and there's this amazing pine scent the air. They make me feel about yea big." He held his finger and thumb about an inch apart.

"Why don't you come out to the garden and help me tidy up a few things, Damon," Dominic suggested. "We'll get away much quicker with two of us doing the chores and in the meantime, Nate and Evrain can pick a route and make lunch to take with us."

"Sure, if that's okay?" Damon turned pleading eyes to Nathaniel.

"Of course. Just make sure you do everything Dominic tells you to. No pulling up things you think are weeds, okay?"

"You can borrow some boots," Dominic said. "My spares might be a bit big for you, but you don't have to wear them for long."

"I'll put on two pairs of socks—they'll be fine."

Evrain smiled, knowing that he probably looked way too soppy, but not caring. Once Dominic and Damon had left, he met Nathaniel's eyes. "I know, I know… I'm a hopeless case when it comes to Dominic."

"He's a wonderful man. I can't tell you what it means to Damon to be accepted here, despite his past. He hero worships Dominic, can't believe that he's been forgiven."

"He was abused, a victim. What Symeon did to him was unforgivable. He's changed a lot under your tutelage," Evrain said. "You're doing a fine job with him."

"I'd got to the stage where I thought it unlikely that I'd ever find a life partner and, at the beginning, I wasn't sure about Damon. He was so…fragile. But he just craved love and attention. Now I can't imagine life without him, so we can be a pair of saps together." Nate lifted his coffee mug in a toast. "Now, how about this hike, where do you think we should go?"

"Well, it's November, so we should probably avoid anything too high up unless you want to be wading through the snow. We shouldn't tackle anything too steep and rocky. We want something level but with good views where we can talk without worrying about taking a header over the nearest cliff. We're spoiled for choice around here. Let me get a map and show you." Evrain extracted a map from the bookcase and spread it on the table. "Here would be good." He pointed to a spot on the map. "It's called a Mirror Lake and on a day like today when there is little wind, you can get an amazing image of Mount Hood reflected in the water. It's a snowshoe hike in the winter — it might be muddy now but there shouldn't be too much snow on the ground. It can get pretty busy, but at this time of year it'll be reasonably quiet. What do you think?"

"Happy to follow your lead on this one. It sounds great and, from the look of it, easily accessible from the highway. Do we need a pass or anything?"

"Yes, we need a north-west forest pass, but we already have one. You can get an electronic day pass now, but Dominic and I venture out enough to make the annual one worthwhile. We just need the one for the car, not per person, so we've got you covered."

"Brilliant, and I suppose we'd better put some sandwiches together or we'll be in trouble. I warn you, Damon has quite the appetite."

"We have enough leftover turkey to feed a small army for a week," Evrain said. "In fact the fridge is full of leftovers. I think there's a whole pie. Considering how much we ate, it's a miracle there's anything left at all, but the fridge is full of boxes that Dominic packed away yesterday."

Nathaniel rubbed his hands together. "Then we have the makings of a great day."

* * * *

An hour later, they were on the road packed into Nathaniel's car, because it was the biggest. Damon and Dominic sat in the back while Evrain acted as navigator for Nathaniel. It wasn't that far from Mount Hood village to the trailhead where they piled out of the vehicle to pull on their walking gear. There was a snap of cold in the air, but the sun was bright.

"It's a perfect day for hiking," Dominic said, shouldering a pack. Evrain had split the lunch between two bags while Nathaniel carried a third containing a flask of hot chocolate and bottles of water. Their burdens would be much lighter on the way back as they intended to picnic by the lake.

Evrain hadn't had much of a chance to talk to Nathaniel before and it proved to be a pleasure discussing Nathaniel's work and how he used his abilities in the management of his windfarms.

"You really found your calling with the air element, didn't you?" Evrain said.

"I was fortunate to find a way I could use my power without the need to channel, though it will be much easier with Damon as my partner. Less exhausting, which means Felix will nag me less about looking after myself."

"It's good to have people around who care for you. What does Felix think of Damon?"

"He likes him, though he'd never say so. He's not afraid to give him a clip around the ear when he needs one either, so there are two of us keeping Damon under control. He's reverting into a brat as he gets his confidence back. To start with, when I took him home with me, he was terrified. He never smiled. Symeon really did a number on him."

"Symeon had the whole bad guy thing written through him like words through a stick of rock. He was rotten to the core and enjoyed being that way."

"There are others like him out there. Power-hungry warlocks who use their gift for their benefit alone. Not on this continent thankfully, now Symeon is gone, but there are some class-A bastards roaming Europe and Asia. It's a good thing we're a rare breed."

"Gregory talked about maintaining a balance. He said I was the fourth corner of the square. Does that mean another warlock will emerge on this continent with Symeon dead and buried?"

"We were three for a long time before you came along. I think the balance was restored when Symeon died. Consider yourself the third point of the triangle instead." Nathaniel grinned. "I shouldn't wish disasters upon us but I'm quite looking forward to us having a chance to work together."

"I hope you haven't jinxed us. Dominic and I would appreciate a quiet life for a while, like a decade or so. Though I suspect it's not likely to happen that way."

"I wouldn't place money on it."

For a while they walked in silence. Evrain watched, amused, as Dominic stopped to point out different plants and birds to Damon, who seemed overjoyed at the attention he was getting. He bounced here and there, tracking Dominic's every move.

"Those two are like excited pups sniffing at every new smell," Nate said. "It's good for Damon to be outdoors somewhere new. He's spent too long in the house. I want to cut back on work and spend some time traveling with him."

"In the States?"

"At first. Then abroad perhaps. I have a very long bucket list of places I want to see and things I'd love to do. Felix needs time to explore his own new relationship. The time feels right, I think. But don't worry, I won't be leaving the US for a long time yet. I won't leave you and Gregory hanging."

"You need to live your life. We could all sit around waiting for the worst to happen. Chances are we won't all be together when it does, anyway."

"True, but I have a feeling...and I can't explain why...that something is about to blow, as it were. I don't think it was coincidence that you were tested so young. Someone, somewhere thinks there's a need for you to be at full strength."

"You may be right. I've been in denial, but I feel it too. Like there's something just out of my line of sight that I can't quite see. The back of my neck itches as if someone's watching me, though I know there's no one there."

"Have you told Gregory?"

"Yes. He was noncommittal, but I think he's worried too." Evrain clambered over a fallen tree. He nodded to a group of walkers heading in the direction they had just come from. "There's quite a few people out today. Shall we catch up to the boys?"

"You're hardly older than either of them," Nate said.

"I feel older."

"Warlocks are born ancient. It comes with the territory." Nate ruffled Evrain's hair. "Don't walk away from your youth too fast. Enjoy yourself—hell, enjoy each other. Life's fleeting even when you live as long as we do. We're not immortal, we could be snuffed out tomorrow. Live every day as if it could be your last — your grandmother told me that once. She lived that way and you should too. Damon has made me see how sound her advice was."

"I miss her," Evrain admitted.

"She was a good woman. Wicked tongue, impatient, but good. I see a lot of her in you."

"I'm flattered." It wasn't a hollow statement. Evrain aspired to be like Agatha. It just felt like a stretch to have the vast amount of knowledge she had accumulated over the years, or the razor-sharp insight and intellect. He chuckled. "You know, with all the bad soap operas she used to watch, you'd think her brain would have turned to mush, but it never did."

"Sharp as a tack was an apt description for her. A tack that would be under the sole of your foot if she thought you'd misbehaved."

"True."

"What are you two getting so intense about?" Dominic asked. "We'll be at the lake soon."

"Good, I'm hungry!" Damon proclaimed.

"You're always hungry, brat." Nate slung an arm around Damon's shoulders.

"Dominic was telling me about all the different kinds of fungi you can find in the forest and that made me think of mushroom stroganoff, mushroom omelets, mushroom soup..."

"We get the picture. There aren't any mushrooms for lunch though. Just cold turkey and cranberry sandwiches and chocolate silk pie."

Damon's stomach growled and he clutched it dramatically. "See? I need sustenance."

"You ate more breakfast than the rest of us put together," Nate growled.

"But, Master, it's your fault I had so much of an appetite." Damon blinked.

"Enough, young man. The rest of the world does not need to hear about that." There were people about as they neared the lake. It wasn't crowded but there was a scattering of brightly clothed hikers of varying ages walking the perimeter of the water. "Wow, I can see why this is a popular spot." Nate took off his pack to extract his camera. "I hope none of you mind if I act like a tourist."

"Go for it." Evrain wandered a little way down the lake shore to a quiet spot beneath the trees. A group of rocks made good seats and a convenient tree stump made a great picnic table. Dominic ambled over.

"It was a brilliant idea to come here. We've been so often I forgot what an impact the view has on first-timers."

Nate was taking lots of snaps of Damon with spectacular scenery in the background. Damon was posing shamelessly.

"I can't believe I'm hungry again." Dominic eyed the packages of sandwiches Evrain had laid out. "I ate so much yesterday."

"It's the fresh air and exercise," Evrain said. He slapped Dominic's hand away from the food. "Hold your horses. We have to wait for our guests."

"Why?" Dominic pouted. "Damon will eat everything!" As he spoke, Damon bounded over.

"Oh wow! Those look so good." He picked a rock to sit on and took the packet Evrain handed him. He stuffed a sandwich in his mouth, spraying crumbs everywhere.

"Told you." Dominic grabbed a packet for himself, scowling at Evrain.

"There's more in the bag. Plenty for everyone." Evrain rolled his eyes at Nate. "Anyone would think they never sat through a huge Thanksgiving feast yesterday."

"That was yesterday," Damon mumbled around his sandwich. "And I'm a growing boy."

For a while, the only conversation involved requests to pass food and pour hot chocolate. Evrain caught Dominic smiling at him and he understood why. He felt peaceful and happy, more relaxed than he'd been in a long while. The way Dominic looked at him was so full of love, made him hot all over, and he had to look away. He didn't want to complete the rest of the hike walking strangely.

Dominic was tidying up the empty sandwich wrappers and Damon was drinking the last of the hot chocolate when a low rumble made everyone look around. The ground shuddered.

"Quake," Nathaniel said, calmly taking Damon's hand.

"We get a lot of them around here," Evrain said. "One or two a week, usually. This one doesn't feel that strong, thankfully."

When the rumbling stopped there was an eerie silence, as if the birds and wildlife waited to see if anything else was going to happen. Suddenly, a whole flock of birds rose from a nearby tree scattering into the sky with agitated cries.

"That could mean another one's on the way," Dominic said. "They know."

They all stayed where they were, waiting. Further down the lake they could see groups of people sitting and standing, glancing around them, expectant.

"Here it comes." Dominic made a grab for Evrain's arm. This time the shaking was much stronger. Small crevices opened in the ground around their feet and the mirror-smooth surface of the lake blurred the reflection of Mount Hood into an impressionist image.

"That one kept going for a while," Damon said, sounding scared. "What's the biggest tremor you've had around here recently?"

"There was a three point one about four weeks ago," Dominic said. "I'd say that was a little stronger. Hard to tell, it could just have been shallower."

"We'll have to be careful walking back," Evrain said. "There will no doubt be some after-shocks." His attention was drawn to yelling where the path met the lake. Two people had run onto the shore, screaming for help. He exchanged a look with Nate and the two of them headed toward the gathering group of people.

"What's going on?" Evrain asked the first person he got to, a young woman in a bright pink jacket and over trousers.

"There was a rock fall just below Tom, Dick and Harry," the woman said. "I think there might be people trapped or hurt up there."

Dominic and Damon had caught up. "What's she talking about?" Damon asked, looking confused.

"Tom, Dick and Harry is the name of the mountain behind us," Evrain explained. "We passed the start of the path to get up there earlier. There are several short spurs that access the lakeshore and a few paths, but it's much craggier on some of the routes. You go so far, to a point that is marked by a huge rock cairn then there's a switch back toward the summit. It's easy at first, along the ridge top but it gets much rockier when you near the base of Harry's summit. The guys that raised the alarm must've taken a shortcut because I think it's about three miles on the main path."

"We might be able to do something to help," Nate said. He walked over to the two men who had raised the alarm.

Evrain waited for him to return. There was no point in both of them getting involved. He was quite willing to bow to Nate's experience and follow his lead. When he returned, Nate's expression was somber. "There is a shortcut, but it's a tough scramble. The rocks came down in the first shake rather than the big one, but the second tremor brought more debris down on top of the original fall. These guys weren't with the group that got swallowed, but they reckoned there were three people, possibly a child. It's going to take a while for any rescue services to get here. I think we should go up there and see if there's anything we can do."

"Agreed." Evrain shrugged out of his jacket. "We'll need to travel light — we'll leave the bags here, take off anything that is likely to slow us down." He took in Dominic's frightened eyes. "Don't worry, love. We'll get there, assess the situation. There may be nothing we can do, we have to accept that, but if there is any chance we can save those people when we're right here on the spot, we must do what we can."

Dominic nodded. He quickly found a spot behind some rocks to stuff their packs and coats. Then, following rough directions given by the two witnesses, they jogged toward the start of the trail.

It took about half an hour to reach the point of the rock fall, which lay at the foot of a steep crag to one side of the path. It was obvious that the fall was fresh, with dust still hanging in the air. Evrain bent over, hands on his knees, trying to catch his breath. The uphill run had been demanding. They had stayed together as a group, slowing when they needed to allow everyone to keep up.

"Can you take a look?" Nate asked. "You're more sensitive to the earth than I am."

"Sure." Evrain sat on the damp ground, removing his gold bracelet. Dominic crouched next to him, his presence lending Evrain strength. He couldn't know who might show up to witness what he was doing so he placed his hands on his knees to keep them still and projected his senses into the ground.

He channeled, sending tendrils of power between the rocks, searching for pockets of air or flows of water. "Three people. Alive. I think they were beneath an overhang, which protected them to a certain extent. I can't tell if they're injured or not but there is a significant mass of rock around them. Getting them out isn't going to be easy." He looked to Nathaniel for direction.

Nathaniel paced up and down, examining the rock fall. Damon, who had come to sit next to Dominic, jerked and moaned. Dominic put an arm around him, steadying him.

"I think I can see a way," Nathaniel said. "At the side of the fall, there's a boulder big enough that if we move it, they'll have a way out from the space they're trapped in. I can probably nudge the boulder enough to give it some momentum, but I'll need you to hold the rocks above where they are, until the people get out. You understand what I mean?"

Evrain nodded. It was a good plan and he could see that it could work, but holding the weight of rock in place would take significant power. "I won't be able to hold it for long," he said, reaching for Dominic's hand. "There's a lot of unstable debris above them. I can create a layer of thick air to protect them, but wouldn't it be better if you did that, Nathaniel? Air is your strength."

"You have a lot more power than I do, Evrain, and a lot more experience channeling through Dominic. I think it's best you do it, if we don't want those people squashed like bugs. I'll deal with the earth."

"Okay. Give me a couple of minutes." Evrain knew full well that Nate was more than capable but he trusted the older warlock to do what was best. He intertwined his fingers with Dominic's, closed his eyes and focused on feeling his way through the rocks. He prayed that there wouldn't be another tremor to shake things loose before he had time to manipulate the air. Muttering under his breath, he coaxed and cajoled the unwilling element to cooperate, building layer upon layer of air until a cushion of protection formed above the void where the three people were trapped. He squeezed Dominic's hand.

"Okay, Nathaniel, Evrain is ready," Dominic said.

Evrain was vaguely aware of Nate working through the earth, loosening the ground beneath the large boulder, encouraging it to shift in the tiniest of fractions. Evrain tensed as the pressure bearing down on his protective air shelf increased. He relaxed his shoulders and let his power flow through Dominic, focusing his will and binding the air in place.

Nathaniel grunted and the boulder moved a few more inches, opening a gap big enough for a person to get through. He ran to the base of the rock fall to peer through the opening.

"Come on, get out!" He pulled the first person from what could have been a tomb. "Quickly, if there's another shock everything could come down on top of you." The woman got clear, then an older child appeared, closely followed by a man with a blood-streaked face. All three staggered clear of the rock fall.

"You can let go now, love," Dominic whispered.

Evrain withdrew his hold on the air as carefully as he could but the moment he relinquished control, an avalanche of rocks and small stones bounced and tumbled to the ground, bringing the overhang with them. The space the family had been huddled in was completely buried.

"There are people coming up the path," Dominic said. "Can you stand?"

Evrain nodded, though his head was pounding. "How's Damon? How are you?"

"Damon is fine. A bit shaky, and I'm perfectly okay. You, however, are white as a ghost."

"You've never seen a ghost, so how do you know?"

"I might have, but that's beside the point. I've seen chalk with more color than you."

"The family, are they okay?"

"Looks like the man has some cuts and bruises but the woman and the boy seem fine. It's a miracle they weren't killed. It would have taken an age to get them out by normal means and I can't see how they could have stopped the rocks collapsing. You did good, love."

"I did, huh?" Evrain didn't feel good, though a deep sense of satisfaction helped alleviate the nausea. "I did what Nate told me to. Where is he?"

"Talking to some guys from the forest service."

"He was right to make me handle the air. His finesse with earth is better than mine, despite air being his strength."

"He knows what he's doing. It might be a good idea for us to get out of here. I don't think there were any witnesses to the miraculous rescue, but you don't want to be answering awkward questions in your condition." Dominic got to his feet.

Evrain took the hand he offered and Dominic heaved him upright. Damon managed on his own though he had a green tinge to his face. "I wouldn't have eaten so many turkey sandwiches if I'd known I'd be the power pipe for windy boy this afternoon."

Evrain snorted with laughter. "There you go, Dominic, apparently you're my power pipe. Oh, and, Damon, I think Nate heard you call him windy boy."

"My ass is grass," Damon moaned as Nate walked across to them.

"It sure is. Later. There's nothing more we can do here and we all need rest. We'll take the easy path back to the lake, collect our stuff then head back to the car. Everyone okay to walk?"

Evrain shivered. Now the adrenaline had left his system he was cold and shaky. Walking would at least warm him up again, even if his legs felt like jelly. "Sure, let's go. I'm craving a fire and hot soup."

* * * *

Two hours hiking followed by half an hour in the car and it was almost dark by the time they got back to Hornbeam Cottage. Evrain had never been so glad to see the old place. Dominic ran ahead to light the fire and put the coffee maker on. Shadow sat on the garden path yowling until they were all safely inside then she jumped onto Evrain's lap the minute he sat down.

"Someone was worried about you," Dominic said. Shadow purred and nuzzled Evrain's chest.

"I'd say she was worried about all of us," Evrain said. The cat gave a meow of agreement before flopping down onto his lap. A minute later, his phone rang in his jacket pocket. "Could you get that, Nate? Apparently it's against the law to eject a cat from your lap."

"Sure." Nate retrieved the phone then handed it over.

Evrain thumbed the screen to connect the call. He held the phone to his ear, then immediately moved it farther away. "It's Gregory... Nate, would you mind?" He handed the phone back with a pained sigh.

Grinning, Nate took the phone. Evrain could hear Gregory's ranting from across the room. When he eventually paused for breath, Nate attempted to get a word in.

"Gregory, it's Nathaniel. I'll put you on speaker, so you're not just giving me earache." He took the chair opposite Evrain, leaving the phone on the table between them.

"What in the hell is going on over there? You two have been slinging your power around left, right and center. Are you all okay? Coryn is unhappy and that makes me unhappy."

"We're fine, Gregory," Evrain said, more to prove he was alive than anything.

"'Fine.' I hate that word. Someone better start with the explanations or I'm driving over there right now."

"There's no need." Nathaniel gave a concise but thorough account of their recent adventures. "Evrain is tired. Damon is now less green, in fact he has his face wrapped around a piece of leftover pie, Dominic has already recovered and I doubt you care much about how I'm doing."

"You've been around the block, Nate. You know better than to overextend yourself. Evrain does not."

"It was a tough ask, but nothing he wasn't capable of. He needs to build up his warlock muscles is all. You have to stop playing around with his training and start taking some risks."

"Apparently. Evrain, I'll text you some instructions…or Coryn will, I can't work my damn phone. They make the keys way too small."

"Thanks for calling, Gregory. Now go back to doing whatever you and Coryn were doing and no, we don't need details." Nate disconnected the call. "That man worries more than my mother. He does know you're all grown up now, right?"

Laughing, Evrain leaned back in his chair. "He's worse since my grandmother was taken from us. She kept me in line. He thinks, and I'm quoting here, that I'm 'undisciplined, lazy and lacking in focus' when it comes to being a warlock. He takes great pleasure in trying to correct my attitude."

"Which is an endless source of amusement for me," Dominic said, bringing the coffee pot and some mugs over. Damon followed with a bottle of Jack Daniel's. "I thought a splash of something warming would do us all good as no one has to drive again tonight. I'll think about feeding us all in a while."

"No, we'll get takeout," Nate said. "I'll go myself. I didn't expend nearly as much energy as Evrain did. I'll take that drink when we get back."

"Yum!" Damon exclaimed. "Can I come with you?"

"You just want to get in the food before anyone else. Don't pretend to be helpful." Nate pulled Damon into his lap. "But yes, you can come so I can keep an eye on you."

Once they'd settled on the easy choice of pizza, Nate and Damon headed out.

"Come here, love. We have half an hour of alone time before they get back." Evrain beckoned Dominic with a crooked finger. After ejecting an indignant Shadow, Dominic straddled his lap, leaning forward for a quick kiss. "You should be resting, not thinking kinky thoughts."

"How do you know what I'm thinking?" Evrain laid a hand over Dominic's crotch.

"I can see it in your eyes and besides, nine times out of ten that's what you're thinking about."

"What about the other time?"

"I'd give that an even three-way split between food, work and warlockery."

"Okay, I'll give you that. Can we get back to kink?" Evrain pictured Dominic naked and bound.

"No. Tell me how you're feeling."

"We're men, we're not supposed to talk about our feelings."

"Evrain…" There was enough warning in Dominic's tone to make Evrain think twice about being flippant. He sighed.

"The fatigue is fading, so is the nausea. I have a slight headache, but that's probably more to do with Gregory yelling at me. Overall, I feel good. It's really satisfying to think I've done something worthwhile—we saved three lives today." He pulled Dominic against his chest. "How about you? I channeled pretty hard."

"You did. But you weren't holding back and I think that helped. You're usually so aware of not trying to hurt me but this time you had to give it everything you had and it was easier somehow. You didn't put your bracelet back on yet."

"Don't need to at the moment. Using that amount of power is draining so I'll be good for a few days. I hate to admit it, but I think Gregory is right. I need to build my magical muscles or the next time something happens I might not have enough fuel in the tank."

"You think there'll be a next time?"

"I know there will. It's a matter of when, not if."

"Yeah, I guess I knew that already."

"Stop thinking about it and kiss me instead." Evrain cupped the nape of Dominic's neck with one hand.

"They'll be back with pizza soon."

"And in the meantime, I have different appetites."

# Chapter Fifteen

A few weeks later, Evrain was leaning against the kitchen counter scooping cereal into his mouth. Dominic appeared at the bottom of the stairs wearing hole-free jeans and a moss-green shirt that made his pale blue eyes stand out even more than usual.

"You look edible," Evrain said around a mouthful of granola.

"Thanks. I think. Are you still okay to drop me in the city? I haven't done any shopping for Christmas and it's only a few days away now."

"I'm done. Got my last gift yesterday," Evrain said, feeling smug.

"That's because you're in Portland most days with easy access to all the stores. I'm up to my knees in muck and unless you want your gift from the general store in town, I need a ride."

"You can buy me lunch. Pete wants to see you so I thought we could all grab a bite together."

"Sure. Then if I'm done shopping, I'll go catch a movie. I can't remember the last time we saw a film and there's bound to be some kind of superhero flick on as the schools are out."

"You just want to ogle men in spandex. I'm jealous. I'd bunk off but I have a big project due in before the holidays and I don't want to have to work during my vacation time."

"Listen to you, you're starting to sound like an American."

Evrain grimaced. "Say it's not so."

Dominic grinned, shrugging into his coat. He bent to lace his boots. "I hope the sidewalks are clear. I hate slithering around."

"The *pavements* have been pretty good. No fresh snowfall for a couple of days has helped and roads in the city are fine now. It's a shame because I'd prefer to be snowed in with you. I can think of plenty of ways to keep warm." *On the rug. In front of the fire.*

"I'll bet you can. Did Shadow have her breakfast?"

"Yes. Spent about ten seconds outside doing her business then shot upstairs. She's in our bed where no doubt her lazy behind will stay for the rest of the day."

"I'm coming back as a pampered cat," Dominic said. "Right. I'm ready. Shall we go?"

"Okay." Evrain got into his outdoor gear. "Ready." In the depths of winter the main disadvantage of living at Hornbeam Cottage was the quarter mile trek along the path to the closest spot they could park their cars. The frigid air prickled against Evrain's skin, his breath clouding every time he exhaled. He didn't mind the cold. The Scottish winters of his youth had been no picnic and he far preferred the process of warming up than attempting to cool down when it was hot. He dug his hands deep into his pockets, wishing he'd remembered his gloves. He warmed in an instant when Dominic linked their arms.

"I love it when it's crisp and cold. Everything's so much sharper and it smells fresh."

Evrain looked anew at the trees, every twig and leaf edged with crystals. The entire world sparkled.

"It's beautiful." He could visualize new artwork for the campaign he was working on. It would mean starting again but he knew it would be better than his current effort. "Damn it."

"Damn, it's beautiful?" Dominic bumped hips with him.

"No...well, yes. You've given me a new idea for something I'm working on and it'll mean starting over. Pete's gonna kill me."

"How, with a Sharpie to the eye?"

"Probably with bad coffee." They reached the car and Evrain got behind the wheel. "Where do you want me to drop you?"

"Somewhere I can shop in the warm." Dominic relaxed into his seat. "Though I don't just want chain stores, so that might be impossible. How about you drop me in Sellwood so I can explore the antique shops then I'll head for Washington Square."

"Nothing will be open in Sellwood yet. It's too early."

"I'll find a coffee shop and hang out for a while."

"Okay. Come by the office when you're done."

Traffic was mercifully light. Evrain dropped Dominic outside a coffee shop before heading into the city. Despite the detour he was in the office by eight and spent a happy hour sketching his new design ideas before Pete arrived around nine. The morning flew by with Pete feeding into the new design ideas with enthusiasm, despite Evrain's misgivings about his reaction.

At two they stood back from the board, hands on hips, mirroring each other's stance.

"It's good." Evrain tilted his head for a different angle. "Crystal dust will make it great."

"It's brilliant. I fully intend to take fifty percent of the credit." Pete gave Evrain a hefty pat on the back.

"You bought decent coffee — you're entitled."

"Cool." Pete's stomach rumbled. "Where's that hotty of yours? I need sustenance."

"Don't call him a hotty, Pete."

"But he is hot. I'm simply stating the truth. No fake news here."

"He is, but no one is allowed to think that but me." Evrain pinned Pete with a stare promising physical damage if Pete didn't retract his statement.

"Everyone thinks he's hot, Ev. Male, female, animal, mineral, vegetable...it's unavoidable."

"Pete..." Evrain's phone vibrated in his pocket. He answered the call with a smile. "Hi, love, you just saved a life."

"What did Pete do?"

Evrain laughed at Dominic's insight. "Failed to connect brain to mouth as usual."

"I'm in the lobby. Am I too late to entice you out for lunch?"

"Not at all. Pete's about to start eating the furniture so your timing is perfect. Give us five minutes and we'll be with you." He ended the call. "You say one word to offend him and I will end you." Evrain gave Pete a smack to the back of the head.

"Hey, that's colleague abuse! Fine...I'll buy you both lunch to make up for lusting after your boyfriend. Let's go to that place on the river Dominic likes, then we don't have to drive. We can even sit outside, 'cause they have huge patio heaters."

"You may have just redeemed yourself with that idea." Evrain grabbed his coat and followed Pete, who was already on his way to the elevator.

When Evrain set eyes on Dominic in the lobby, his entire body temperature rose by a few degrees. Dominic was flushed, his cheeks and nose pink from the cold. His hair was wind-tousled, tucked into the turned-up collar of his overcoat, and his feet were surrounded by bags. Three paces and Evrain was able to draw Dominic into his arms for a welcoming kiss.

"Holy shit, you two are hot. I should sell tickets." Pete fanned himself. "Hey, Dominic."

"Hey, Pete." Dominic waggled his fingers in greeting.

"Do you have a death wish?" Evrain glared at his friend. "I swear I will…"

"Take me for food. That's what you're going to do." Dominic hooked his arm into Evrain's.

"Pete's paying for lunch. We're gonna walk over to Pier 13 on the waterfront."

"I love their burgers!"

"And I want hot chocolate with cream and marshmallows. It's Pete's buck so I'm going all out. You can leave your shopping behind the reception desk." Evrain attempted to peek into a bag but Dominic whisked them away from under his nose to stash behind reception.

With Pete grumbling alongside them, they made the short walk to the restaurant. Many of the outside tables were taken but Pete, moving with a speed Evrain had never witnessed before, snagged a great spot when a family got up to leave.

"Check out the menu and I'll go order at the bar," Pete said. "I know what I'm having."

"Cheese and chili burger with all the fixings, curly fries on the side," Evrain and Dominic chorused together.

"So sue me for choosing the best thing on the menu." Pete licked his lips.

"Chicken fillet burger for me," Dominic said. "With a side salad. Can we get some nachos to share while we're waiting?"

"Good plan. I'll have the house special, Pete," Evrain said. "Garlic wedges. And don't forget my hot chocolate."

"I'll have one of those too, thanks, Pete," Dominic added to the order.

"Did you just bat your lashes at him?" Evrain accused Dominic. "Do not encourage him."

"Pete's fun. I like him and so do you."

"He wants you."

"You think that about every man I've ever met, and most of the women."

Evrain glanced around the surrounding tables. Several people were casting covetous looks at Dominic. "That's because it's true."

"Have you ever considered that it might be you they're looking at?" Dominic grabbed for the napkins as a sudden gust of wind picked them up and shook the umbrellas providing some shelter from the elements. "Calm down!"

"Hey, look!" a woman at the next table shouted. "There's a tidal bore coming down the river."

Dominic watched, open mouthed, as a ridge of water swept along the river, lifting boats and creating a wash along the banks. "It's not a bore," he whispered. "It's going the wrong way."

"Must be a flash flood," Evrain said. "Heavy rain in the mountains, no doubt." He affected innocence, not easy considering the knowing look Dominic sent his way. "I don't like people eyeing you like you're a juicy steak ready to be eaten."

"That doesn't mean you should get excited. I don't see them, I see you. Only you."

"Sorry?"

"You don't look sorry. You look far too pleased with yourself."

"Got them watching something else, didn't I?"

"Gregory will have your hide."

"What Gregory doesn't know won't hurt him."

"He'll have felt the surge, won't he?"

"He'll just think I'm being good. Practicing like I'm supposed to."

"I'm not gonna win this, am I?"

"Nope." Evrain leaned back in his chair. "And I'll be reminding you again who you belong to when we get home tonight." Dominic's blush made him smile.

"What did I miss?" Pete asked, returning to the table with a tray of mugs. He dished out hot chocolate. "Someone came inside shouting about a wave on the river."

"It was a bit of a surge is all," Evrain said. "Flash flood."

"I miss all the good stuff." Pete took his seat. "That kind of shit can make you a YouTube gazillionaire if you catch it on film. Food will be about fifteen minutes. The kitchen's rammed." He took a huge slurp of his chocolate. "Wow, that's good."

Evrain shrugged out of his coat. The patio heaters were blasting warm air and his recent exertions had already warmed him up.

"So when are the three of us gonna have a night on the town?" Pete asked. "I need to get laid and you two are a honeypot for all the buzzy gay bees. One or two might want to pollenate me when they realize you two are off limits. We can even go to a den of kink if you want to."

"Den of kink?" Evrain spluttered into his chocolate. "You want to find yourself a nice, strict Dom to make you behave, Pete? Or perhaps a sweet sub to worship your comic collection?"

"Funny. Hey, what's that?" The wail of sirens broke through the chatter, heading their way. They all turned so that they could see the nearest road, which led to a bridge across the river.

"Police," Evrain guessed.

A black sedan with tinted windows came into view, weaving erratically through the traffic, closely followed by a Portland PD patrol car. Brakes squealed as vehicles attempted to get out of the way.

"Crap, he's going way too fast. There's a work crew on the road before the bridge..." Pete stood to get a better look along with most of the rest of the restaurant's clientele. "Shit...the safety barriers along the bank are down where they're working."

There were gasps and screams as, just before it reached the bridge, the sedan hit a ramp, clipped the road crew's barricade then somersaulted into the river. The patrol car swerved violently, avoided the road workers by inches but caught a curb then rolled over and over before following the sedan off the edge.

"Fuck!" Pete craned his neck for a better view. "We should go help." Four more police cars arrived on the scene and a crowd gathered on the riverbank.

"We'd just get in the way," Dominic said.

"Stay between me and everyone else," Evrain said, grabbing Dominic's hand. He focused, gathering air and dragging it beneath the surface of the river. The Columbus was huge and powerful—the water didn't want to cooperate, churning, flowing fast, dragging at the invading machinery. Evrain sought the metal, surrounding what he hoped was both vehicles with pockets of air, forcing the water out. He gripped Dominic's hand, the direct connection between them helping him channel. Holding the shape of the air below the water took immense effort but he could think of no other way to help. One metal mass began to rise. Evrain drew more air into the bubble, encouraging it to move, and the cop car popped to the surface. He slowed the current, fighting the river's will. Sweat beaded on his forehead despite the chill.

"The cops are out, swimming against the current," Dominic said. "There's a rescue boat heading their way."

Twisting his free hand into a new shape, Evrain let go of one air bubble and focused on bringing the other car to the surface. He was exhausted and had to reduce the amount of air around the vehicle. Bubbles exploded on the surface of the water.

"I can't hold it much longer." In desperation, he channeled harder. Next to him, Dominic tensed.

"River police have arrived. There are divers getting into the water, Ev. Not much longer." Dominic kept his voice low. His calm soothed Evrain's panic. Then he lost it. His hold on the elements slipped and the air pocket fragmented into thousands of tiny bubbles. The water flow increased. He sagged into the nearest chair, his vision gone.

"They got them," Dominic cried. "Two men. They're both in the boat. So are the cops."

Evrain took long, deep breaths. He felt like he'd run a marathon or three and every muscle he possessed ached. Something wet dribbled from his nose.

"You're bleeding!" Dominic pressed a wad of paper napkins to Evrain's face.

"Can't see," Evrain mumbled. A glass touched his lips and he took a long swallow of water. Slowly his vision changed from black to red to white then cleared. He wiped his nose, hiding the bloody paper in his fist. Dominic came to sit next to him. "It's over. Everyone got out of the water. I don't know what you did, but it worked."

"Good. That's good. Did anyone notice?"

"No. Too busy rubbernecking the action. You're very pale."

"Has my nose stopped bleeding?"

"Looks like it." At that moment, a server showed up with their food, which brought Pete back to the table.

"That was some excitement, huh?" He shoved his sandwich into his mouth. "If they'd gone off the bridge the drop would have killed them. They were lucky air pockets formed when they went in as well or they'd all be fish food."

"Is that what happened?" Dominic asked, pushing Evrain's plate toward him.

"Must have been. One car floated up and then you could see the air from the other one coming up in bubbles. Water was churning. Wow, it was like something out of an action movie. All we need now is for Bruce Willis to show up."

Evrain mustered a brief laugh. He chewed his food, savoring every mouthful as his energy returned enough that he felt less like an extra from *The Walking Dead*. He got through lunch on a combination of willpower, bluff and Dominic's unstinting support as he kept Pete engaged in conversation.

Evrain's burger could have been compressed sawdust, but the hot chocolate nudged his taste buds back to life. By the time they were done eating, it was almost three-thirty and Evrain had no intention of going back to work, even though he felt a lot better. He and Pete agreed to call it a day so after retrieving Dominic's shopping from the office, they all scuttled down the back stairs to the underground parking lot.

"I feel like a naughty schoolboy playing hooky," Pete said.

"We've done enough overtime to merit an early afternoon every now and again," Evrain said. "I feel no guilt."

"Promise me we'll get together for a smexy night out soon."

"Smexy? No. Just for using that word we aren't going anywhere with your sorry ass."

"Aw, come on, Evrain. You know you want to."

"We'll sort something out," Dominic placated him, brushing off Evrain's protests. "He'll plague you until you agree anyway."

"I will." Pete grinned. "You should always listen to Dominic. He's cleverer than you and far sweeter." He ran to his car.

"You best run... Shit, I'm too tired to chase him." Evrain leaned against his car. "You'll have to drive, love."

"No, really? You're dead on your feet." Dominic waved to Pete as he drove toward the exit. "Get in the car. Home, bath and bed is what your future holds."

"Has potential," Evrain murmured. The car journey would be long enough for him to recover. Once they got going he slipped into a doze, his head filled with the ways in which Dominic would make him feel all better.

# Chapter Sixteen

Dominic lay on his front, chin propped in his hands. He tangled his feet with Evrain's, who was propped against his pillows reading one of Agatha's old books.

"My handprints look good on your ass," Evrain observed, leering.

Dominic twisted to look but, other than some pink edges, couldn't see. "I'll have to take your word for it."

"Aren't you cold? Get back under the covers."

"No. You warmed me up. The cold air on my skin is nice." Evrain had held him down, fucked him then spanked him. He'd enjoyed every minute and was relaxed enough to accept that he didn't need to understand why. Languor weighted his limbs and he had no desire to move. "It's allowed to be lazy on Christmas Eve, isn't it? I don't want to move." He was answered not by Evrain but by the bedroom door being nudged open. A dark, furry head poked around it. Shadow gave an annoyed meow before leaping onto the bed. Dominic scrambled beneath the covers before Shadow's claws could make contact with his bare skin.

She stomped up and down the bed, rubbing her cheek on the corner of Evrain's book, patting his hand and nosing at Dominic's chest.

"Someone wants her breakfast," Evrain observed.

"And I suppose you think I should be the one to get it?" Dominic wriggled deeper beneath the comforter. "She's huge. She'll last till New Year's on her fat reserves."

"No, I will. I intend to pamper you over the holiday so breakfast in bed can be your first treat." Evrain stretched before giving Shadow a good scratch under the chin.

"I'm so glad we decided to stay here and have Christmas with just the two of us," Dominic said. Shadow gave an indignant yowl. "Okay, three of us. I love our friends but it's such a luxury to have three whole days to ourselves. I got everything up to date in the garden and the greenhouses so I'm all yours for the whole holiday."

"You're all mine regardless." Evrain slipped out of bed then pulled on some jeans. "Don't move."

"Don't intend to." Dominic winced as Shadow used his stomach as a launch pad for a flying leap toward the door. He admired the lines of Evrain's back and the little divots above his ass. Evrain seemed to achieve his toned muscles with little effort whereas Dominic's came from hard labor in the garden. Not that he minded. The thought of being trapped in a gym gave him the shakes. He guessed that using his elemental powers gave Evrain quite a workout. He was always exhausted when he'd been channeling and ate like a horse afterward but never gained a pound. He smiled. Thinking about Evrain made him happy. He loved every inch of his weird, possessive, dominant boyfriend.

The muted sounds of conversation drifted up the stairs. Dominic couldn't make out the words but Evrain often held full-scale debates with Shadow, who seemed to understand every word. She articulated her responses through a series of noises and physical reactions and Dominic had no doubt that something of Agatha's spirit resided in the cat. He chuckled. He lived with a warlock so a possessed cat was hardly a stretch.

He dozed, enjoying the luxury of a rare lie-in, until Evrain returned with a laden tray, which he placed on the bed. "Get started while I go for the coffee. I couldn't carry everything in one go."

By the time Evrain returned, Dominic had sat up with the tray of food balanced on his lap. He reached for the coffee Evrain offered to find himself presented with a gift-wrapped parcel.

"What's this? It's not Christmas until tomorrow." He shook the parcel but there was no rattle to give away the contents.

"You can open it after breakfast. It's something to keep us entertained today."

"Will it stop me doing some Christmas baking?"

"Nope. Now eat your breakfast because I can't wait to see your face when you open it."

Evrain had produced creditable French toast, a plate of sliced fruit and a dish of natural yogurt. "This is great." Dominic ate slowly, guessing that the gift was more for Evrain than for him and this was the one chance he would get to torture him rather than the other way around. He took his time savoring a strawberry. "So sweet."

"Unlike you. I know what you're doing." Evrain took the tray away. "No more coffee until you open your gift."

"That's unusually cruel, even for you." Dominic grazed the back of Evrain's hand with his fingers. "But I'll bite. What did you get yourself?"

"I have no idea what you mean."

"Riiight." Dominic tore the paper from the present to reveal a flat, square box. He removed the lid then parted black tissue paper. Nestling inside was a leather collar, an inch deep, with a heavy buckle fastening. He lifted it from the box and a chain dropped from a metal loop attached to the leather. At its end was a smaller loop of leather. Dominic took it in, his cock hardening.

"You'll wear it for me." It wasn't a question. Evrain's certainty was absolute.

"Will I?"

Evrain traced Dominic's neck with a finger. "It's going to look so good wrapped around your throat. You can wear jeans today, but no shirt. I want to see the chain disappearing below your waistband, knowing where it's going. Every time you move the chain will tug the strap around your balls and you won't be able to come. Not until I allow it."

Dominic gulped. He wanted to protest, to deny that Evrain's description excited him. "No." He didn't mean it.

"Oh yes, my love. Your entire body is screaming yes. Gonna plug you. Keep you ready for me."

"You're dreaming."

"This is one dream that's going to come true."

"I need to…" Dominic made to get out of bed but Evrain rolled over him, pinning him down.

"You don't need to do anything. You can't run from your desires, sweetheart."

Dominic squirmed beneath him but rubbing against Evrain's hard body did nothing to alleviate his arousal. Evrain went to his knees and unzipped his fly. His cock sprang free and Dominic was fixated. He couldn't look away even if he wanted to.

"Suck me." Evrain crawled over him until he could press his cock to Dominic's lips. He grabbed the headboard. "Open."

Dominic parted his lips, desperate to taste, but this wasn't about his pleasure. This was Evrain taking what he wanted, but he didn't, not straight away. Instead he leaned down to adjust the pillows under Dominic's head, positioning his head at a better, more comfortable angle. The irony of his care wasn't lost on Dominic.

"Softy."

"Shut up." Evrain's dick proved to be an effective gag. "Just because I don't want you to get a crick in the neck does *not* make me soft." He punctuated his words with repeated thrusts into Dominic mouth. All Dominic could do was lie there and take it. "You'll wear my collar because I want you to. You'll keep my plug inside you because I demand it." Evrain stiffened, the vein in the side of his neck throbbed and his eyes flashed. He came in a hot gush down Dominic's throat, gripping Dominic's hair with one hand and the headboard with the other. He thrust a final time before withdrawing with a hum of approval. "Do we understand each other?"

Dominic licked a dribble of cum from the corner of his mouth. "You made yourself clear, love." He reached for his aching cock only to have his hand slapped away.

"Oh no. No fun for you. Not yet. When I say so, not before."

"You *are* feeling dommy this morning."

Evrain clambered off the bed. "I'm me." He grabbed the collar, slipped it around Dominic's neck. "Sit up so I can buckle this."

Cold at first, the leather soon warmed against his skin. It felt strange but not uncomfortable. The chain dangled against his chest, the links clinking.

"Now for the good bit. Lie back." Evrain pushed the covers down to Dominic's ankles. The chain pulled taut as Evrain fastened the leather strap at its end around the base of Dominic's cock and balls. "Very nice." Evrain tugged on the chain. "Does anything pinch?"

Dominic shook his head. "I'm not sure about this."

"I am. Hands and knees."

Sighing, Dominic got into position and the chain slackened. He rested his head on his arms. There was nothing to stop him unbuckling the collar. He only had to ask and Evrain would remove it, but that wasn't what he wanted. The need to please Evrain overruled every other thought in his head. Slick fingers probed his hole, closely followed by the blunt end of a plug. Ridged marble penetrated his channel, filling him, the sensation keeping him erect. Evrain played with it a little, teasing him.

"Will you stop already! It's Christmas—you're not supposed to be mean."

"This isn't mean." Evrain pushed the plug all the way in. "This is giving you, and me, a lot of pleasure." He gave Dominic's ass a smack. "Put your jeans on. I want to see what you look like."

"I'm gonna stay in bed all day." A large part of Dominic wanted to hide.

"You're supposed to be baking. You promised me gingerbread men and you were going to make my mum's spiced biscuit recipe."

"That was before."

"I'll give you a choice. Either you can get up and bake me goodies with your jeans on, or I'll keep you naked all day and edge you until you scream."

"Remind me why I love you?" Dominic reached for his pants.

"No idea. It's a complete mystery to me." Evrain leaned in for a kiss. "You, me, eggnog and baked goods — it's going to be a perfect day."

Dominic wasn't so sure but he dressed in jeans and thick socks anyway, tucking his erection away with a pained sigh. When he stood straight, the chain attached to his collar tugged the strap around his balls. Every movement reminded him that he was bound for Evrain's pleasure.

"That looks hot as hell," Evrain observed. "I love the hint of what's going on that can't be seen."

Dominic stomped down the stairs without commenting. He needed a distraction from the physical reactions of his body so he started pulling ingredients and utensils from cupboards and drawers. He had a tried and tested recipe for gingerbread so he intended to do that first. Once the figures had cooled he'd let Evrain do the decoration. It would keep him out of mischief.

"Why are you smiling?" Evrain settled in a chair at the kitchen table, scanning the messages on his phone. "Gregory texted me a list of exercises to perfect but I filed them under 'go away'." He flicked his fingers at the fire and the flames roared higher. "Wouldn't want you to get cold."

Dominic kept quiet. It wasn't as if Evrain really expected an answer. He had a tendency to ramble when there was a lot going on his head.

"Fuck. I want to bend you over the table right now."

Dominic shivered. "That wouldn't be sanitary and besides, I'm busy." He held up flour-coated hands. "And so should you be. Gregory will know you've been slacking."

"Spoilsport. Bake quicker, then you won't have an excuse."

"Why don't you make some more coffee?" Dominic suggested, flouring a board ready to roll out his dough. "It's a bit early to start on the eggnog." He watched Evrain move. Even something so simple as making a pot of coffee showed off his innate grace. He moved with more elegance than Shadow. Dominic's cock jerked and he sighed—he should learn not to let his thoughts stray. He stamped out two baking sheets worth of gingerbread men then slid them into the oven. "Fifteen minutes and they'll be done."

"Then sit with me and have coffee," Evrain said. "I have dibs on the first gingerbread man." Dominic went to take a seat but was pulled into Evrain's lap. "I love the smell of baking."

"Cats and cakes make a place home—that's what my great grandma used to say."

"You make this home, love. Wherever you are, I'm home."

"Soppy warlock."

"Must be the festive spirit taking hold." Evrain pulled Dominic down for a kiss. "Or that I'm the luckiest man on the planet." He pulled at the chain running from Dominic's collar.

Dominic gasped. "Stop that!"

"Why?"

"Because."

"Because what?"

"Because you're making me…"

"Oh, I do hope so."

"You're incorrigible."

"And you sound like my grandmother. She used that word a lot, often before smacking me around the head."

"Which I'm sure you deserved."

"Probably."

"Definitely." Dominic leaned against Evrain's chest. "You make me feel so…I don't know. Loved isn't the right word. Protected, cherished. I mean, I know you love me but it's more than that. It makes me want to please you."

"And you do, all the time. You're a submissive… Your faith in me is an honor. You trust me with your body and you give without hesitation. You're part of me."

Dominic didn't want to ruin the moment, but it was time to get his biscuits out of the oven. He slipped from Evrain's lap, evading the grab Evrain made for him. "Once these have cooled you can decorate them." Dominic took the cookie sheets from the oven then moved the gingerbread figures onto wire cooling racks. "I'm going to start your mum's recipe now." Evrain pouted. "Do you want biscuits or not?"

"It's a shame you can't cook from my lap. You look sexy as hell and I want to play with you."

"Playing leads to burning and I'm not sure even your special skills can rescue charcoal biscuits. Besides, you should be practicing."

"Fine. Do you mind if I channel?"

Dominic shook his head. "Of course not, go ahead." He focused on the recipe, ignoring the aches in his muscles as Evrain got to work. He had four jars in front of him on the table, one half filled with earth, another with water. One seemed empty but obviously contained air and the last, a tea light, its flame sparking with excitement. Evrain's green-gold eyes flashed and his fingers danced as he manipulated the contents of each jar in turn. Dominic could feel a slight vibration through the table and he watched, fascinated, as bubbles rose through water and the earth in the jar shaped itself into the figure of a cat, chasing its tail. The candle flame burned silver then blue and the jar of air rocked as a miniature whirlwind formed inside it.

Dominic was entranced. He wanted to praise Evrain's efforts, but didn't dare break his concentration. He went back to baking, rolling his shoulders to ease the twinges. Once the trays were back in the oven, he sat quietly at the table, trying not to fidget as the plug inside him shifted. He knew the moment Evrain stopped channeling because the growing pain in his muscles subsided. The contents of the jars returned to their usual innocuous state and Evrain sighed.

"That's tougher than it looks."

"It was an impressive display," Dominic said. "I could watch you for hours."

"Are you done baking, because I really want to make better use of this table?" Evrain got up, moving to stand behind Dominic. He massaged his shoulders, kneading away the tension. He slid a finger beneath Dominic's collar then pulled his head back by the hair, leaning over him for a kiss. A bolt of lightning shot through Dominic's groin and he worked the plug with his inner muscles until Evrain released him.

"Over the table. Now."

Dominic stood and Evrain dragged the chair away. He tore at Dominic's jeans until they fell to the floor and he was able to kick them away. Evrain pushed him down onto the flour-covered table, holding Dominic's hands behind his back in one hand. With the other he delivered two sharp smacks. Dominic spread his legs in blatant invitation.

"Such a slut."

"For you, yes."

Evrain fumbled with the plug, pulling it free then tossing it into one of the armchairs by the fire. "I'm developing a fetish for you in socks and nothing else, though this"—he tweaked the chain between Dominic's collar and cock ring—"is suitable adornment." The sound of a zipper, followed by some jerking and shuffling, told Dominic that Evrain had managed to get out of his pants. Seconds later, Evrain pushed inside him. The well-lubed plug had kept him slick but there was still an initial bite of pain.

Evrain wasn't gentle. He seemed barely under control as he pistoned his hips. His grip on Dominic's wrists tightened and Dominic's cheek rubbed against the well-worn wood of the table.

"Evrain, please…I need to come. The strap…" Evrain groped beneath Dominic's body. It took forever for him to undo the buckle, cursing as it refused to come free. A burst of power dissolved the metal and the strap fell away. He gripped Dominic's aching shaft in one hand, held his wrists with other, then pushed deep into his body. Dominic came with a scream, sending pulses of cum into Evrain's fist. Evrain let go of his wrists, grabbed a handful of hair then came, pulling Dominic's head up from the table.

"Fuck!" He pounded into him twice more before collapsing over him. "Feels like Christmas came already."

"I think we both came." Dominic pushed up, hinting for Evrain to get off him. He was breathless, sweaty and happy. "I need to clean up, I have flour everywhere!" He shook his head, creating a white cloud. "I'm gonna take a shower." He turned off the oven. "Would you take that last batch out of the oven for me? I've put out another wire rack for them to go on."

"Sure, though I can't promise there won't be a few missing by the time you get back." Evrain stood, unbuckling the collar around Dominic's neck.

"No doubt." Dominic grabbed his discarded pants and padded toward the stairs. He put an extra wiggle in his hips. "Leave some for me." He ran when Evrain made a lunge for him.

Dominic smiled and hummed through his shower. When he dressed he pulled on a soft pullover over his jeans. If Evrain wanted him half naked again he'd have to say so. Dominic hoped for cookies and cuddling in front of a movie, the glow of candlelight and the twinkle of fairy lights from their small Christmas tree. He chuckled at his romantic musings.

When he got downstairs there was no sign of Evrain. The kitchen was full of the rich scent of melted chocolate, which Evrain had been using to decorate the gingerbread men. When he saw his efforts, Dominic burst out laughing. Each biscuit had been 'dressed' in various kinky outfits, including collars and cuffs, harnesses and thongs. "It's a good thing these are just for us."

Evrain came through the door that led to the small snug-come-TV room, phone pressed to his ear, his expression a mixture of determination and frustration.

"Yes. Yes, Gregory, we'll be there. I know! You don't have to remind me." He disconnected then pressed the phone to his forehead. "Damn it. I'm so sorry, love. Christmas is canceled. We have to get to San Francisco."

"When? Why?"

"Now I'm afraid. I'll have to explain on the way."

"Okay."

"Just okay?"

"If you say we have to go then we have to go. I'll set up the automatic feeder for Shadow. Do you know how long we'll be gone?"

"A day or two at most, I hope. You sort things down here. I'll go throw a few things in an overnight bag." He took Dominic's hand and gave it a squeeze. "I love you."

"I love you too. Together, remember. Whatever this is, we're in it together."

Evrain kissed him, lingering as their lips met, the contact chaste but intimate.

Dominic tried not to panic as he packed up cookies and organized food and water for Shadow, who appeared from the snug, parked on the hearth rug and licked a paw. She seemed utterly unconcerned by the flurry of activity.

"I guess this is how it's going to be, Shadow," Dominic said. "Warlock business trumps Christmas festivities. I have a bad feeling about this."

"Me too." Evrain dumped a holdall next to the table. "Are you ready?"

"As soon as I get my coat and boots on."

"You're being amazing about this." Evrain frowned. "Today of all days."

"I don't suppose the elements care that it's Christmas Eve. They misbehave when they feel like it, not when it's convenient." Dominic shrugged into his warm coat.

"Sounds like you," Evrain said, grinning.

Dominic rolled his eyes. "Cheeky warlock. Let's go before my courage fails me." He leaned into Evrain's side and silently prayed that they would both make it home intact.

# Chapter Seventeen

From a small, private airport outside Portland to San Francisco by private plane, with no delays, took less than ninety minutes. When Evrain and Dominic deplaned, Nathaniel's driver, Felix, was waiting for them, the car parked on the taxiway.

"Gregory must have pulled some strings to arrange all this," Dominic observed, climbing into the back seat of the car. Evrain got into the front next to Felix.

"Actually, I imagine Nate has more pull around these parts." He twisted to make sure Dominic was settled.

"And you'd be right," Felix said, pulling away. "Mr. Alberich has a lot of powerful friends. It's good to see you both, albeit not under the best of circumstances."

"You too, Felix. Still keeping Nate and Damon in order?"

"Mr. Alberich is manageable. Young Damon, however, has 'brat' tattooed on his backside." He sounded fond despite his words.

"He is unique, that's for sure," Evrain said.

"That's one way of putting it," Dominic added. "So where are you taking us, Felix? Gregory only gave Evrain the scantest information over the phone."

"I'll leave Mr. Alberich to explain, but we're heading south of the city along Highway 280 to San Andreas Lake."

"San Andreas...should I read anything into that?" Evrain's stomach knotted.

"I wouldn't like to say, but the others are already there. You two are the last to arrive."

"Others?"

"Mr. Alberich and Damon, Gregory and Coryn, Killian Archambault and Eric."

"Killian, why is that name familiar?" Something niggled at the back of Evrain's mind.

"The test. He was the warlock on Skye," Dominic said.

"What the hell is he doing here? I hoped I'd never have to set eyes on him again."

"All I know is that Mr. Alberich was relieved when he found out he was in the country. We'll be there soon."

Evrain scowled. He hated not knowing what was going on. "Has there been much earthquake activity in the area recently?"

"The usual rumbles," Felix said. "But there were a couple of bigger shakes yesterday. A way off shore, but enough to bring in a small tsunami. Nothing to cause significant damage."

Evrain closed his eyes, taking deep breaths. He had a feeling he was going to need all his strength in the coming hours. Dominic leaned over the seat to squeeze his shoulder and he placed his hand over Dominic's. His fingers were cold despite the warmth of the car.

Felix turned down an access road and the ride got rougher. It was already dark, and hard to see much of the surrounding scenery.

"The lake isn't open to the public because it's part of San Francisco's domestic water supply, connected by aqueduct to our water source in the Sierra Nevada near Yosemite," Felix said, expertly guiding the car down the narrow track. The lights and noise of the highway faded into silence as he followed the fence line to a set of high gates topped by razor wire.

"Here's where I leave you. Mr. Alberich told me to drop you off then drive home, but I'm staying. I won't be far away. I'd prefer you don't mention that to him."

"Deal." Evrain shook Felix's hand before getting out of the car.

"The gates are open. Good luck."

Dominic came to stand next to Evrain and they both watched as Felix reversed the car down the track. When the lights disappeared, they turned to the gate and Evrain took Dominic's hand. He opened the huge gate just wide enough to admit them then closed it. "No point in drawing attention to our presence, I suppose, though I doubt anyone would be coming out here on Christmas Eve in the middle of the night."

Dominic squeezed his hand. "Where do you suppose the others are?"

"No idea, but there's only one path and it has to lead somewhere." They began to walk, treading carefully in the darkness. "Dom, if whatever this is goes wrong…"

"Don't say anything else. It's not going to go wrong."

"But if it does." Evrain pressed a finger to Dominic's lips to stop his protests. "You will do whatever it takes to be safe. Do you understand? I need to know that you'll do what I ask." He replaced his finger with his lips, giving Dominic a gentle kiss. Dominic's full-body shudder perked Evrain's dick into action. He leaned forward, pressing his forehead to Dominic's. "This is the most ridiculous time to get excited."

"If it makes you happy, I'll do as you ask, but if it comes to it, and I can't, you must promise to do the same. No sacrificial heroic nonsense, okay?"

"Okay. I love you, but if we don't get moving, I won't survive Gregory's temper, let alone whatever has brought us all here."

"I think the name of this lake is a pretty big clue," Dominic said, his tone wry.

"I'm afraid you're right."

The path hugged the edge of the reservoir. There was no wind to disturb the surface of the water, which was so black it could have been a hole in the earth rather than a lake. A jet passed high overhead and Evrain watched its path, wondering at how people's normal lives were continuing all around them. He had to accept that normal would be forever out of reach for him and Dominic.

"There's a building over there," Dominic said, pointing out a dim low shape in the distance. "It probably houses some machinery to do with the reservoir, but I can't see where else we need to go."

Evrain nodded. "And I think I just spotted a light." A flickering beam steadied, pointed in their direction, then moved toward them. "Someone is coming out to see where we are."

They walked quicker and out of the darkness, Coryn appeared, wielding a large flashlight.

"Finally! I got sick of Gregory's pacing, so came to find you. Felix rang to say you were here."

"Hi, Coryn. It was quite a long walk from the gate and we didn't have a torch," Evrain explained. "Neither of us fancied a dip in the lake so we took our time."

"Come along inside where it's a fraction warmer, at least. Hi, Dominic, sorry we had to ruin your Christmas Eve."

Dominic smiled and shrugged. "It's the same for all of us."

Evrain led the way into the building. To one side a tangle of huge pipes and machinery whirred, the white noise somehow comforting. To the other, his friends were gathered on an assortment of mismatched chairs positioned around a battered table.

Damon immediately bounced over to give Dominic a hug. "Come and sit by me. I'm kinda scared."

Gregory gestured, pointing out an empty seat for Evrain, who nodded at the assembled group. Coryn came to stand at Gregory's shoulder. Nate leaned across the table to shake Evrain's hand. "Thank you both for coming so quickly."

"Evrain, I need to introduce you to somebody you've met, but don't know," Gregory said. "This is Killian Archambault and his partner, Eric."

Killian gave him a small bow. "It's a pleasure to meet you under less trying circumstances, young man."

Eric smiled, but didn't speak. He was slight, round metal glasses balanced on the end of his nose, his head topped by a mop of messy chestnut-brown hair. Killian was a complete contrast. He was tall and broad shouldered. His hair was shaved close to his scalp and he sported a neatly cropped beard. Everything about him, from his expression to the way he held himself oozed dominance. Eric pressed clung to his arm, clearly besotted.

Evrain was tempted to come up with a sarcastic retort but settled for a nod and a slight smile.

"Killian and Eric were visiting New York for the holidays. We were fortunate they were in the country," Nate said.

"What's going on?" Evrain asked. "I feel like I'm a few steps behind the pace here."

"I'll explain," Gregory said. "One of Nathaniel's duties in this area is to periodically check the status of the fault lines. He travels enough around California managing his windfarms to make it an easy enough process. Every six months or so he visits the main hotspots and feels for potential problems."

Evrain understood what that meant — he was familiar enough with casting his elemental senses through the earth when he helped Dominic in the garden. He couldn't imagine what it must feel like to sense the contained power of the fault lines.

"And I'm guessing he found something worrying on his latest tour?" Evrain asked. The slight lines around Nathaniel's eyes were deeper than usual.

"Indeed. Something deeply troubling. Nathaniel, perhaps you would care to explain?"

Nate nodded. "Of course. I should give you some background, first, so apologies for the geography lesson. The lake we are next to was originally a small natural sag pond. Do you all know what that is?"

"No clue," Dominic said.

"When tectonic plates slip and create a natural V-shape in the land, water often gathers to form a pond. The lake here was expanded by the construction of a hundred-foot-high earth dam in 1868. It's something of a miracle, but the dam survived the 1906 earthquake intact despite the fact that the fault line runs directly beneath it."

Damon looked beneath the table as if searching for cracks.

"The lake was named after the fault. It's a hotspot for seismic activity and always on my checklist, mainly because of the dam. The last big quake happened out at sea. If the epicenter was directly beneath us, the dam wouldn't survive and the damage would be catastrophic, not just from the water.

"So what did you find?" Evrain asked.

"The best way for you to understand is for you to feel for yourself. Gregory and Killian have already taken a look because I wanted other opinions about what I suspected. I can't describe it. You need to take a look for yourself."

Evrain nodded. "It would be easier for me to be outside." He didn't need to be in direct contact with the earth to feel what was going on beneath the surface, but it made things simpler. He beckoned to Dominic. "Give us a few minutes."

Evrain led Dominic down to the lakeshore. He didn't say anything, and Dominic didn't ask any questions, for which he was grateful. He cleared his mind and focused his senses on the lake, probing the black depths until he found rock. He channeled, closing his eyes to reduce distraction. The instability of the fault line was immediately obvious, but he got the sense that it had been that way for an age, settling with a groan every now and again like an old man with arthritic joints. He widened his range, probing into hidden nooks and crannies and found a spot that glowed angry red in his senses. This had to be what Nate had discovered. The enormity of the plates was overwhelming and Evrain had to channel hard to narrow his focus. He was aware of Dominic tensing next to him, but he had to put Dominic's pain out of his mind while he listened to the earth. Abruptly, he cut off, pulling Dominic into his arms for hug.

"That's enough, let's get back inside." They re-joined the others around the table.

"Well?" Gregory asked.

"The pressure down there, it's terrifying," Evrain said. "I sensed a minor fault, branching from the main one where two sections of rock are grinding against each other. The structures can't hold. There's going to be a slip and it's going to be a big one. I could hardly comprehend the scale of what's going on down there, but it burned dark red in my mind. Whatever is going to happen is imminent. If we're going to attempt to do something about it, it has to be now. The epicenter is so close to the surface. I can't imagine what the level of destruction would be."

"We've all come to the same conclusion." Gregory sighed. "Your view is more detailed. Do you have any ideas for a solution?"

Evrain hadn't expected to be asked for his opinion. With three much more experienced warlocks in the room, he imagined his place was to be told what to do and then do it. His surprise must have shown on his face.

"Remember, Evrain, that since you passed the testing you are the most powerful of all of us. If it weren't for you, I wouldn't even consider attempting to do anything about this," Gregory said. "I've told you before that it isn't always possible for us to intervene where the elements are concerned. A tweak here and there is all that we've been able to accomplish. The depth of your abilities means that we can explore more radical work, and I'm not assuming that we will succeed, but I think we have to try."

Evrain nodded. "Of course."

"Any warlock visiting this country has to let me know about their presence, which is how I knew Killian was in New York. His deepest affinity is with earth, so we are very fortunate that he and Eric are here and willing to help."

"Our pleasure," Killian said. "Any of you would do the same if I needed your help in Europe. But even my connection to the earth is not as deep as Evrain's. I'd be very glad to hear your thoughts, young man."

"I think there might be a way." Evrain reached for Dominic's hand, needing his support. "It'll take all of us, though, and it isn't going to be easy. I'll be honest, I'm not sure I'm strong enough for what I have in mind."

"Let's hear it." Nathaniel steepled his fingers and leaned forward. Killian pulled Eric onto his lap.

"We need to play to our strengths. Gregory will need to extract all moisture from around the area I need to work in. I'm not even sure it can be done that far underground."

Gregory shrugged. "I can certainly give it a try."

"Nathaniel will then need to create cushions of air so that the plates don't move before I'm finished with what I have in mind. Killian, I'll need you to loosen the structure of the rock, then I'll use the heat being generated by the friction between the plates to fuse the rocks together." Evrain looked at the faces around the table. "You think it's ridiculous, don't you?"

"I think it's...ambitious," Killian said. "But not impossible. In simple terms, what you're suggesting is a kind of elemental glue. What do you think, Gregory?"

"It might just work. The idea is simple though the execution is complex. I think I can do my part. Nathaniel, what about you?"

"It'll be a challenge. I've not been channeling through Damon for very long and not with the kind of intensity this is going to need."

"I can take it," Damon said, white faced. "This could save thousands of lives, couldn't it?"

"Hundreds of thousands," Gregory clarified. "And billions of dollars in damages." He tapped his fingers on the table. "It's decided—we'll give Evrain's idea a try. If we fail, the situation won't be any worse than it was before."

"Unless what we're doing sets something off," Evrain said.

"Well, you will have to make sure that doesn't happen," Gregory replied, his expression grim.

As they all walked out into the night, Killian took Gregory to one side. "You're putting an awful lot of weight on those young shoulders, Gregory. Are you sure he's up to it?"

"No," Gregory admitted. "How could I be? Nothing like this has ever been tried before."

"The strain could kill him. His part is by far the hardest of all of ours."

"You've seen him in action, Killian. In the heat of it, so to speak. I train him as best I can, but I have to let go of the reins and now seems an appropriate time, don't you think?"

"If he thought the testing was a baptism of fire, he'll be learning new lessons tonight."

"I think we all will."

They reached the lakeshore and arranged themselves in a loose circle, each warlock standing close to his partner. Coryn looked anxious, Damon pale as a ghost, Eric determined—he had removed his spectacles. Dominic was trying to hide his anxiety, but it wasn't working. Evrain tried to give him a reassuring smile but he feared it reflected his own insecurity and fear.

"Let's get started." He had Killian to his left and, though he didn't know the man, took comfort from his strength.

Coryn shuddered as Gregory raised his arms and began invoking the first stage of the plan.

# Chapter Eighteen

Evrain closed his eyes and extended his senses into the earth. He could see, or rather sense, the slow but steady movement of water as Gregory drew it from the pores of the rock. As each droplet was removed from the area of the fault line that Evrain meant to fuse, it was replaced by a miniature cushion of air. Nathaniel's control was impressive. To keep so many different spots in his head and maintain the integrity of the protection he was providing was an immense task. Damon whimpered and Evrain took a quick look to see him sagging against Nate's side. Nathaniel lowered him to the ground then knelt next to him, muttering and twisting his fingers into complex shapes, never stopping. Damon's face was twisted in pain and Evrain had to close his eyes again. It was too hard to watch.

Gripping Dominic's hand in his right, he bent the middle finger of his left hand until it touched his palm. He twisted his thumb in the opposite direction and extended his remaining fingers. The ache in his hand from the unnatural position helped his focus. Power flowed through him, or rather through Dominic as his conduit, into the ground. He probed deeper and deeper, following the path laid by Nathaniel and Gregory. He sensed Killian working alongside him, not yet manipulating the earth, just getting to where he needed to be.

In Evrain's mind, the area where there was most friction between tectonic plates burned red hot. The heat was so much more than anything he had dealt with before—even the magma Killian had produced during his test was cool in comparison. The tension between the rock faces was immeasurable and, for a moment, he was terrified of what he was attempting. His confidence faltered. As if sensing his uncertainty, Dominic stroked the palm of his hand with his thumb. The gentle, rhythmic movements calmed him. Next to him, Killian grunted and deep beneath the earth rock fragments and crystals began to shift, creating a substance that Evrain could work with.

Pushing aside the pain in his head, Evrain muttered a rapid series of words, weaving his fingers into complex shapes as he sought to gather the heat contained within the earth. He wasn't sure how he knew that he had seconds to act but he was absolutely certain that if he failed, catastrophic events would follow. He threw every ounce of energy he possessed into controlling the fire element, pulling molecules together, encouraging the heat to rise and rise. He replaced Nathaniel's air bubbles with liquid heat, dissolving the mobile crystals Killian had created into liquid rock. He was shocked into opening his eyes when a geyser of steam and rock erupted from the surface of the lake, sending fragments of superheated granite high into the air. As they landed, every particle created a hiss. None of the debris was close enough to hurt his friends so he ignored the noise and carried on pouring power into the fault line. He hadn't thought about how he would cool the liquid rock to fuse the plates together and there was no way he could control the other elements at the same time, but Gregory, Nathaniel and Killian came to his rescue. He released his hold on fire as cool air and cold water doused the massive area of liquid rock. The reaction hit him like a bus, throwing him off his feet as the fire element tried to push back. It wanted to grow, to create more heat, and Evrain got the sense that it blamed him for being thwarted. The angry backlash whipped across his body in a line of fire, pain consumed him and white light filled his vision. It was as if his entire body burned on the lakeshore and when darkness came, it was a merciful release.

Evrain was still channeling until the moment he hit the ground. Dominic caught him as he fell, dropping to his knees to cradle Evrain's body. He didn't dare say anything as it was apparent that the other warlocks were still engaged with whatever was happening deep below the surface of the earth. Evrain's face was flushed and sweat coated his brow even though the temperature had to be below freezing. His left hand was clenched into a fist and when Dominic massaged it, he found blood oozing between Evrain's fingers. Under layers of clothing, he couldn't tell if Evrain had further injuries, but his breathing was fast and ragged. Dominic was desperate to get him somewhere safe where he could check him over properly but he had to wait.

Gregory swore and leaned heavily against Coryn. His skin had an unnatural gray cast to it and he looked exhausted. Nathaniel took a deep, shaky breath. His eyes, which had darkened to black, cleared. In his arms, Damon was barely conscious. Nathaniel stroked his hair with a trembling hand. Eric seemed dazed but was peppering Killian's face with kisses and muttering soothing words to the warlock whose drawn face betrayed his pain.

"Did you succeed?" Dominic asked.

"Yes." It was Nate who responded. "Evrain fused a massive area of rock. I don't know how he did it. How is he?"

"Alive. Apart from that, I don't know." Dominic's voice shook. He was close to tears and desperately trying to hold himself together for Evrain's sake. "I need help getting him inside."

"I think I can manage that." Killian extracted himself from Eric's grip. "You grab his feet and I'll take his head."

Between the two of them they carried Evrain inside, laying him on the floor with a rolled-up coat to cushion his head. Dominic started checking him from the bottom up, shoving his hands under Evrain's clothes to check for injuries. He pushed up his pullover, opened his shirt and cursed when he saw the livid mark crossing Evrain's body from hip to shoulder. He could have been slashed with a flaming whip.

"Fuck." Dominic had no idea what to do. He couldn't think.

Killian dropped to his knees next to Evrain's body. "Fetch me some water, Eric. There's a small kitchen area over there."

Eric found a sink with a single tap and in the cupboard beneath it there was a bucket full of cleaning supplies. He tipped everything onto the floor then filled the bucket before lugging it across to Killian.

"Here."

"Perfect." Killian pulled Evrain's shirt further apart. He cupped his hands in the bucket then spooned water across Evrain's wound, muttering under his breath as he did. Ice crystals formed on Evrain's skin and his breathing eased.

"Need to get the heat out of the wound," Killian said. "You keep adding water and I'll keep freezing it. It doesn't take too much energy."

After a few minutes of the unorthodox treatment, some of the redness around the wound had faded and Evrain's breathing had evened out—as if he were sleeping rather than unconscious. Killian staggered to his feet then slumped into a chair by the table. From somewhere, Coryn had managed to magic up hot water, a jar of coffee and some mugs and was handing out hot drinks. Every man in the room seemed shell-shocked.

Evrain coughed and his eyes flickered open. "Fuck, everything hurts. Did I get trampled by a passing water buffalo?"

Dominic snorted his laughter, relieved that Evrain was able to see the funny side of the situation. "Actually, I think you just saved a lot of people from a terrible fate. No water buffaloes were involved."

"Indeed," Gregory said. "And nobody outside the few of us will ever know about it."

"Can you make it to a chair?" Dominic asked, propping Evrain up little.

"Why am I half naked?"

"That's where you're going?" Dominic said. "Killian did some warlock first aid on you. You should be grateful."

Evrain probed at the wound across his chest. "I felt that happen. Thought I'd been sliced in half. Some kind of backlash." He staggered to his feet and, with Dominic's help, collapsed into the nearest chair. "Is that coffee?" Coryn pushed a mug toward him. "I think I deserve a brandy, but this will have to do."

"You were incredible tonight, Evrain," Nathaniel said. "I've never seen so much power so finely controlled, and the scale of what you achieved was immense."

"I couldn't have done it alone. It was a team effort."

"One that saved hundreds of thousands of people and billions of dollars," Gregory said. "Not a bad night's work."

Damon coughed, then moaned. "I'd rather take three of Nathaniel's spankings than go through that ever again."

"You'll take them anyway," Nate growled. "You did good, brat." He stroked Damon's hair.

"It hurt," Damon whined. "Please, let's not do this again anytime soon."

"I sincerely hope that won't be necessary."

"Good." Damon settled against Nate's chest. "Oh, and happy Christmas everyone."

When Dominic checked his watch, it was two in the morning. "Happy Christmas." They clinked mugs in an impromptu toast.

There was a knock on the door and before anyone could react, it opened. Felix stood there, hands on hips. "I'd quite like to make it home before dawn if that suits you all."

"Felix, I told you to go home once you'd delivered Evrain and Dominic," Nate said.

"You did and I didn't. Deal with it. The car is at the gate along with another chauffeur-driven limousine, so get your behinds in gear and move. How you imagined you'd find transport at this time on Christmas morning, I'll never know. All brains and no common sense."

"Succinct as always, Felix," Gregory said. "Though I for one greatly appreciate your disobedience." There was a general murmur of agreement.

"I love you, Felix," Damon said, eyelids drooping.

"Me too," Eric echoed. "I was thinking we might have to hitchhike back to the city. It's a shame warlocks can't fly, or levitate, or do that thing like on *Star Trek*."

Killian cast a sharp glance at Felix, then to Nate.

"It's okay, Felix is fully aware of what we are, Killian," Nate said. "Perhaps, if everyone can manage it, we should follow him before he gets impatient."

In the general move toward the door, Dominic took Evrain's arm and much of his weight. "It's not far, love, then you can rest." He kissed him. "Merry Christmas."

He and Evrain brought up the rear of the procession back along the edge of the reservoir. It seemed so tranquil and, as Dominic gazed across the water, he could hardly believe that the scene hid such potential for catastrophe. A crisis had been averted while people slept peacefully or enjoyed their Christmas festivities. Midnight Mass had gone on undisturbed. A deep sense of accomplishment filled him. The worth of Evrain's power became ever more evident and he was proud to be a small part of it.

"What are you thinking about?" Evrain murmured.

"Completely random things," Dominic said. "Like how I grew sage for our turkey stuffing and now it won't be used."

"Hmm, I don't believe you for a minute but regardless, we'll have our Christmas a day late when we get home. I have some more...inspiring gifts for you."

"I'll bet you do." Dominic gave Evrain's ass a cheeky pat. "I'm sure Santa has delivered some interesting things for you too."

# Chapter Nineteen

Evrain shifted in his seat, pulling the pile of blankets closer around him. It was a sharp, clear night and very cold, but this was how Dominic wanted to see in the New Year, so he'd have it no other way. The garden swing seat had been a Christmas gift from Gregory and Coryn, delivered not long after Evrain and Dominic had returned from California. Positioned at the back of the cottage, in the shelter of the eaves, it gave a view of a wide expanse of sky and tonight the celestial show was spectacular.

Dominic rounded the corner of the house, well-wrapped up in a down jacket, fleece-lined sweats and a woolen hat. His nose was pink and his cheeks flushed.

"Here." He handed over a mug of hot chocolate. "I thought this would be better for a toast than champagne."

"Are there marshmallows?" Evrain swirled a spoon through the rich mixture.

"Do I ever leave them out?"

A few pink blobs floated to the surface of Evrain's drink. "Just checking."

Dominic snuggled beneath the blankets next to him, rearranging a few cushions to get more comfortable. He leaned against Evrain's chest with a contented sigh.

"I wish you didn't have to go back to work tomorrow."

"But I do." Evrain played with a lock of Dominic's hair. "And we had a great Christmas, despite everything, didn't we?"

"We did. It was good of Nate to put us all up."

"It was fun." Evrain had slept until late afternoon on Christmas day, as had the other warlocks, but Dominic, Damon, Coryn and Eric had recovered quicker and between them, produced a Christmas feast for that evening. "And you had a chance to get to know Eric better."

"He and I are going to keep in touch. He wants to start his own herb garden and I promised to help him."

"Killian wasn't as bad as I expected him to be."

"Well, you didn't meet under the best of circumstances, did you?"

"He's powerful. He worked miracles that night at the lake."

"But not as strong as you."

"I'm not sure that's a good thing."

"It is what it is. You can't do anything about it so there's no point worrying. Drink your chocolate."

Evrain smiled at the order. Dominic had been coddling him since Christmas day and Evrain had enjoyed being taken care of. Not that he needed it. He'd been tired to the point of exhaustion and the wound across his body had hurt more than he'd admitted but it had healed fast, leaving only a faint, silver line as a reminder.

"It's almost midnight." He gazed at the stars — innumerable glittering pinpoints of light in a black velvet curtain. "This sky makes me feel small. It puts things in perspective."

"Yes, it does." In the distance the church clock began to chime the hour. Evrain put his mug on the ground then guided Dominic's head to get access to his lips.

"Kiss me." Dominic leaned in, lips parted. As the New Year arrived they were sealed together, everything else forgotten but the connection between them. Evrain let the kiss linger, not wanting to lose the contact, but Dominic pulled away. He wriggled from beneath the blankets then held out a hand.

"Take me to bed."

"Sounds like a great way to welcome in the New Year."

Hornbeam Cottage was warm and cozy, the fire sparking as Evrain walked past. He calmed it with a word, the effort needed now so slight he hardly noticed what he was doing.

"You've changed since that night," Dominic said, leading the way up the stairs.

Evrain could have argued but he knew it was true. "I think a little part of me had been resisting the power. I wanted to keep a piece of myself apart, but that night it wasn't possible. There was no room for barriers. It's part of me and I have to accept it."

Shadow, who must have been sleeping on their bed, strolled by with a green-eyed glare.

"That told us!" Dominic laughed. "You know, it didn't hurt nearly as much as it should have done... I mean when you channeled that night. The power you had to use… I was prepared for it to be agonizing, but it wasn't."

"I'm glad." Evrain stripped Dominic slowly, relishing the reveal of every piece of bare skin. He wrapped his fingers around Dominic's erection. "I'll never tire of touching you." He gathered a twist of air and used it to brush Dominic's balls.

"I should hope not." Dominic rose on his toes. "Why are you still dressed?"

"Because this way, you're at my mercy." He thickened more air, using it to push at Dominic's hole. Dominic whimpered.

"Stop that!"

"I don't think so." Evrain gave Dominic a gentle shove, pushing him down onto the bed. "Keep your legs spread."

While he took off his clothes, Evrain played with the air, caressing every sensitive spot Dominic possessed. When he was bare, he knelt over him, engulfing Dominic's cock with his mouth. Dominic bucked and Evrain narrowly avoided bruised lips. He licked and sucked until he had Dominic writhing beneath him, begging for release.

"No. I want you to come while I'm inside you." He lifted Dominic's calves onto his shoulders. "Damn…lube."

Dominic groped beneath the pillows, extracting a half-empty tube. Evrain grabbed it. He slicked his cock with economic movements—too much pressure and he'd come.

"Hurry…"

"Patience, love."

"You're a wicked tease. There's air doing Lord knows what to my ass and I'd much rather it be you up there."

Chuckling, Evrain pressed the head of his cock to Dominic's hole. A thought sent a spiral of air around Dominic's shaft, constricting the base. "I'm as impatient as you are..." He thrust home with a grunt, marveling at the heat of Dominic's body. "Every time is new. Never the same." He jacked his hips, unable to move slowly. Need overtook him.

"Harder... Won't break..." Dominic's voice cracked. He raised his arms over his head to grasp the headboard.

Evrain took Dominic at his word. He gripped his hips and gave his desire free rein. The rush of emotion that always came when he made love to Dominic threatened to overwhelm him. He threw his head back and cried out as he came, shuddering threw his orgasm. Belatedly he released his mental grasp of the air, allowing Dominic to follow him with a cry. He grabbed Dominic's cock, pulling him through his release with a few swift jerks.

Evrain collapsed next to Dominic and for a few minutes they both lay there, breathing heavily. "That was a perfect start to the New Year," Evrain said, reaching for some tissues to clean them both up. He pulled the covers over them. "In the morning I'm going to lock you in the new chastity tube I got you for Christmas — it'll give me something to dream about all day at work."

"You got that thing for you, not me." Dominic snuggled close, throwing a leg over Evrain's thighs. "I'll just have to make sure you're so late in the morning you won't have time to think about it."

"What do you have planned for the day while I'm slaving over a hot drawing board?"

"To have a think about the year ahead in the garden. It's too cold to do much else but the larger greenhouse needs cleaning out and I'd enjoy the exercise."

"Now you've got me thinking about you, all hot and sweaty, streaked with dirt...yum." Evrain pulled Dominic on top of him. He knelt, the covers falling from his shoulders. "Ride me."

"How are you good to go again already?" Dominic batted at Evrain's cock, making it sway.

"Elemental warlock, remember. The body *is* over fifty percent water." Evrain grinned. "And my control has improved exponentially."

Dominic leaned down for a kiss. He abandoned Evrain's lips for his chest, kissing his way the length of Evrain's scar. "How about we make this the year when you don't get damaged? I don't want to be afraid for you all the time."

"I wish I could make that promise," Evrain said, winding his fingers into Dominic's hair. "But I can't. Let's be satisfied that we can be happy now. In this moment. Even I can't control what the future brings, however much I might want to." He tugged Dominic's head up. "Okay?"

"Yes." Dominic smiled. "With any luck we'll have a drama-free year."

As he settled himself onto Evrain's cock, Evrain smiled. He doubted it would be the case but, for now, being joined to the man he loved was enough.

# Want to see more from this author?
## Here's a taster for you to enjoy!

# The Retreat: Serving Him
### L.M. Somerton

### *Excerpt*

"Who'd have thought there would be so many applicants for a role where the job description includes nudity and a willingness to get your arse whipped?" Carey Hoffman leafed through the pile of paperwork in front of him. "This is a lot harder than recruiting for club servers."

"Relax, Sir. It's important we find the right people. The more applicants we get, the better chance we have of finding someone perfect." Alistair Easton, Carey's submissive, kneaded his Master's shoulders. "Our first paying client deserves the best."

"That's so good." The tension melted from Carey's shoulders as Alistair loosened knotted muscles. "Maybe we should go upstairs for an hour so that you can relieve other parts of my anatomy."

Alistair giggled. "Not a good idea if you want to invite people in for interviews this week. We have work to do."

Scowling, Carey turned to his friend and bar manager Harry Croft. "What's a Dom to do, Harry, when his sub takes charge?"

"Generally," Harry replied, "I find it's best to do what I'm told." He ruffled his sub's hair. Kai Smithson was seated on the floor between Harry's legs. "You can always spank him later, but for now, Alistair is right. We have to get through all these applications this evening. We only have one post left to fill, don't we?"

Alistair knelt at Carey's side, hands folded in his lap, his serenity in complete contrast to the noise and activity going on all around them. The Underground was always busy, but Friday nights tended to be hectic. Carey had sequestered a quiet corner for their discussion. A low table held paperwork and drinks, and cushions softened the floor for Alistair's knees and Kai's backside. Carey still found it hard to concentrate. He blamed Alistair for looking so tempting in leather trousers and a sheer silk shirt. He imagined removing the shirt, exposing Alistair's smooth skin inch by inch, then watching his lover wriggle out of the trousers…

"Carey?" Harry brought him out of his daydream.

"Sorry, I got a bit distracted. Where were we?"

"The last vacancy — if you can keep your mind on recruitment and off whatever it is you're planning to do to Alistair?" He shared a conspiratorial grin.

"Oh, yes. Right. Well, I'm thankful Mr. Wilder's requirements are not too onerous. Tor Halvorsen will act as executive chef. He cooked for Joe and Heath when they had their taster weekend with Olly and Aiden and their reviews of his cooking were first rate. Olly said, and I'm quoting here, that Tor's double chocolate brownies were better than an orgasm after two days in chastity."

Alistair and Kai both burst out laughing.

Harry rolled his eyes. "Olly would be proud. He can create chaos even when he's hundreds of miles away. That's two extra strokes for you tonight, young man."

He gave Kai's hair a gentle tug. Kai sucked on his lower lip but his eyes sparkled and he rubbed his cheek against Harry's thigh.

"Tor has recruited two kitchen assistants, both, I might add, stolen from here at The Underground," Carey said. "As Mr. Wilder is traveling alone, Tor says that will be more than adequate to cover his stay and allow for days off for each of them. Tor intends to work through and take some time off in between clients. He'll also take on training Benjy and Frank. Going forward, I think we should consider rotating the junior kitchen staff through The Retreat. Then they'll all get experience of different kinds of catering."

"That's a great idea. At least they won't be shocked by anything they see at The Retreat." Harry grinned. "Right. Goran has sorted all the drink supplies, so Mr. Wilder won't starve or go thirsty." Goran was Harry's very capable deputy bar manager. "He can always take a quick trip down there if Tor needs him for anything. It's always possible that the client will want to throw a party while he's staying. Goran's already offered to run the bar for events like that."

Carey nodded. "Excellent. Then we have Luke Redding as general manager. He's ex-forces, like Tor."

"The Retreat is going to be run like a military campaign," Harry said. "Tell me about Luke. I know he's a member here but not much else."

"He's a well-respected Dom. Kept up his membership even when he was overseas on active duty."

"Well, you do give service personnel an excellent discount."

"I do, and they deserve it. Whereas Tor was in the army, Luke is ex-Navy. Served fifteen years then took an honorable discharge to care for his father who died last year. Mother passed when he was a child so his dad brought him up. He told me at the interview that he gave himself to his career, then to his father, now it's his time. He was very open. He doesn't have to work for the money but needs a purpose. He's a very experienced manager and won't take shit from anyone. He'll be perfect for mentoring the young men that will be working at The Retreat, as well as the contractors. Management of the house and garden staff as well as all the arrangements related to housekeeping and maintenance will sit with him, and if our guests want any training in a particular technique, Luke can either handle it himself or bring someone in from the club if he doesn't feel qualified. He knows the area well too — he was based at Portsmouth for many years and the New Forest was a favorite daytrip destination."

"I hope I'll get to meet him one day," Harry said. "I'm surprised I've never come across him here."

"I'm sure you will. I intend to have post-stay debriefings with The Retreat's management team here at the club."

"Good idea. So, when you Skyped with Mr. Wilder…"

"Lorcan. He prefers to be called Lorcan."

"When you Skyped with Lorcan, did he have any special requirements for other staff?"

"I think he's going to be a low maintenance client — he was reserved, but friendly. The stay is a personal reward for selling his business. From what I could make out, he's done little else but work for many years. He's had some training as a Dominant and has excellent references from a couple of clubs I know in the U.S. He wants to see whether immersion in the lifestyle is what he wants because, as he said, he thinks it is but he's never had time to prove it to himself."

"Sounds like he has his head in the right place."

Nodding, Carey flicked through a few applications. "I've done a full background check. There was an incident in his late teens, which I won't go into here because it shouldn't cause any issues. It marks him as a survivor. He plays hard when he has the time but that isn't often. He admits to a preference for blonds. Smaller than him and not too muscled."

"How tall is he?" Harry asked.

"Six feet one."

"That rules out three of these — all within an inch of that height. There are also several brunets and one redhead in here so I'll put them aside. That still leaves six possibles."

"Whoever we choose has to be prepared to be very flexible." At Harry's feet, Kai giggled. "Not that kind of flexible, brat," Carey chided. "Lorcan wants one man to be his personal assistant, valet and submissive. He doesn't want a lot of people around the place because his break is about getting some breathing space, so this man will be at his beck and call twenty-four seven. Experience isn't needed. I think Lorcan wants someone he can mold to his requirements, so we're looking for a relative innocent — but one who knows what he's getting into."

"And who understands the difference between furniture wax and candle wax." Harry rolled his eyes. "Talk about mission impossible."

"The housework will be light, just Lorcan's bedroom and bathroom. The contracted cleaning service will handle the rest. We'll need someone bright enough to be an effective assistant…"

"And who doesn't mind taking notes naked, with a plug up his arse." Harry laughed. "Sorry, I'm being facetious."

"You may not be that far off the mark. Nudity and minimal dress are nonnegotiable."

"Well, that helps us narrow the field a bit more. Two of these applicants are house subs here. I know them both and I don't think either of them could be called sweet and innocent—they're a pair of brats. Of the remaining four, two have university degrees and one went to work straight from school but got very good grades at A level. The last one seems to have drifted from job to job but does have waiting experience."

"Drop him for now and ask the other three to come in. When we have time, I want to see all the applicants we've rejected for this job in case they'd like us to hold their details for future opportunities. It would be nice to be able to offer clients a portfolio of staff to choose from rather than having to go through this process all the time. That way we can also broach the subject when we recruit staff for The Underground. Whoever we choose this time will be permanently employed, but The Retreat is fully booked for months. We'll need to alternate between clients so that the houseboys can take some time off and that means we need to line up someone else for the next booking after Mr. Wilder. We can cover unexpected illness or, God forbid, walk-outs, with staff from the club in the meantime." Carey caught Alistair's eye. "What do you think, love?"

"The catalogue is a brilliant idea. I'd be happy to take pictures for it, but maybe you should ask some of the members what they think, too? You have an instant audience for research here."

"You're right, of course." Carey surveyed his club. The Underground was his pride and joy and he fully intended to make The Retreat just as perfect. "I'll leave the interview arrangements to you, Harry. Time for me to make sure my members are happy. I think the boss giving his sub a public spanking might go down well tonight, don't you?"

"You know it will."

At Carey's side, Alistair shivered. Carey stroked his hair. "Would you like that, sweetheart?"

"If it makes you happy, Sir." Alistair kept his eyes downcast but Carey could see he was smiling.

"Oh, it will, you can be sure of that and if you're very, very good you might even get to come. Emphasis on the *might*." Carey raised his glass. "A toast. Here's to finding someone for Lorcan Wilder who lives up to our exacting standards."

Harry pulled Kai onto his lap. He clinked his glass against Carey's. "Bottoms up!" He avoided spilling his drink by the narrowest margin as Kai shook with laughter.

"They soon will be." Carey chuckled while Alistair tried, unsuccessfully, to conceal a groan.

PUBLISHING

Sign up for our newsletter and find out about all our romance book releases, eBook sales and promotions, sneak peeks and FREE romance books!

# About the Author

Lucinda lives in a small village in the English countryside, surrounded by rolling hills, cows and sheep. She started writing to fill time between jobs and is now firmly and unashamedly addicted.

She loves the English weather, especially the rain, and adores a thunderstorm. She loves good food, warm company and a crackling fire. She's fascinated by the psychology of relationships, especially between men, and her stories contain some subtle (and some not so subtle) leanings towards BDSM.

Lucinda loves to hear from readers. You can find her contact information, website details and author profile page at https://www.pride-publishing.com